A Night for Us

A Wilder Brothers Prequel

Carrie Ann Ryan

A NIGHT FOR US

A WILDER BROTHERS PREQUEL

By

Carrie Ann Ryan

A Night for Us
A Wilder Brothers Prequel
By: Carrie Ann Ryan
© 2022 Carrie Ann Ryan
eBook ISBN: 978-1-950443-73-4
Paperback 978-1-63695-166-9

Cover Art by Sweet N Spicy Designs

Praise for Carrie Ann Ryan

"Count on Carrie Ann Ryan for emotional, sexy, character driven stories that capture your heart!" – Carly Phillips, NY Times bestselling author

"Carrie Ann Ryan's romances are my newest addiction! The emotion in her books captures me from the very beginning. The hope and healing hold me close until the end. These love stories will simply sweep you away." ~ NYT Bestselling Author Deveny Perry

"Carrie Ann Ryan writes the perfect balance of sweet and heat ensuring every story feeds the soul." - Audrey Carlan, #1 New York Times Bestselling Author

"Carrie Ann Ryan never fails to draw readers in with passion, raw sensuality, and characters that pop off the page. Any book by Carrie Ann is an absolute treat." – New York Times Bestselling Author J. Kenner

"Carrie Ann Ryan knows how to pull your heart-strings and make your pulse pound! Her wonderful Redwood Pack series will draw you in and keep you reading long into the night. I can't wait to see what comes next with the new generation, the Talons. Keep them coming, Carrie Ann!" –Lara Adrian, New York Times bestselling author of CRAVE THE NIGHT

"With snarky humor, sizzling love scenes, and brilliant, imaginative worldbuilding, The Dante's Circle series reads as if Carrie Ann Ryan peeked at my personal wish list!" – NYT Bestselling Author, Larissa Ione

"Carrie Ann Ryan writes sexy shifters in a world full of passionate happily-ever-afters." – *New York Times* Bestselling Author Vivian Arend

"Carrie Ann's books are sexy with characters you can't help but love from page one. They are heat and heart blended to perfection." *New York Times* Bestselling Author Jayne Rylon

Carrie Ann Ryan's books are wickedly funny and deliciously hot, with plenty of twists to keep you guessing. They'll keep you up all night!" USA Today Bestselling Author Cari Quinn

"Once again, Carrie Ann Ryan knocks the Dante's Circle series out of the park. The queen of hot, sexy, enthralling paranormal romance, Carrie Ann is an author not to miss!" *New York Times* bestselling Author Marie Harte

A Night for Us

Eli Wilder is at a loss. Due to tragedy, time, and life in general, he and his five brothers are suddenly getting out of the military at the same time.

Only none of them have any idea what to do next.

Eli might have a plan—one so far-fetched it will take a miracle for them to agree to it.

When he takes a chance, however, he meets the perfect woman. One he hadn't expected.

Now he has one night to prove he's the right man for the job—and for her.

Chapter One

Eli

Home is where the heart is. Or maybe just where you rest your boots after a long day. A long week. Hell, a long twenty years.

I wasn't even forty years old yet, and here I was, retired. Or at least as retired as one could be after putting in twenty with the military. I had put my entire life and career towards one goal, and now I was out. There was no going back. I was never going to work for the military again as a civilian or get a GS—general scale—position. I was just me...in this house I was renting because I wasn't sure where I wanted to live, but it was my home for now.

My boots were in the closet, scuffed and worn, and most likely headed towards the trash pile.

But I wore my new boots, ones that I was just now wearing in, getting to fit around my feet. And I had a roof over my head, and I suppose my heart was in it. Therefore, this was home.

I pinched the bridge of my nose and let out a breath. I clearly needed more coffee if I was going to pick apart a saying and add poetry of my own.

"Why did you ask us over here if you're just going to growl at yourself the whole time?" Evan asked from the doorway into the kitchen, and I turned to see my brother standing there, his posture rigid, slight lines of pain around his eyes. He was still getting used to the new prosthetic, but with therapy and a whole shit-ton of doctors, Evan was able to stand here in my kitchen on his own accord, with a glare on his face. Of course, the glare had always been there, even before the IED.

"Seriously though, are you going to come in with the rest of us? We got the barbecue."

"From Harmon's?" I asked, my stomach rumbling.

"Of course we got it from Harmon's," Everett

called out from the living room, and I snorted before grabbing the six-pack of beer I had for this occasion.

I followed Evan out of the kitchen and into the living room, where Everett, Elijah, East, and Elliot were already lounging. We could have sat in a dining room, but I didn't have a large enough table for us. So we would be sprawling on my worn couch and used armchairs. I hadn't been able to get furniture of my own all my life. Or at least my adult life. I had moved from place to place, starting out in the barracks, and then I used rented furniture from the military because I was either overseas or living on base. When I had moved off base, I had put most of my money away and hadn't bothered with expensive furniture. Now I had furniture that I got from thrift stores and garage sales. Most guys I knew my age and rank had household items that didn't look like they belonged to a young bachelor. But all of them were married and had families. I'd run from mine.

"What is with this couch?" Elijah asked, sitting nearly ramrod straight at the edge of it. "We're adults now. Shouldn't you have something that isn't so brown and lumpy that you can sink into?"

Evan grunted as he sat into the armchair, resting his leg straight out in front of him. "This chair isn't that bad, but it's not good."

I flipped them both off as I handed everybody a beer and took a seat on the floor. I may be the eldest here, but my brothers had already claimed the chairs, so I was stuck with this. "Honestly, I was just thinking that I needed new shit, but first, I need a house. One that's not a rental."

"It's still a good time for the market," Elliot put in, looking down at his phone. He bounced his foot quickly as he spoke, and I held back a snort at that.

"I know it's a good time in the market." That was a decent segue, so I let out a breath. "However, I don't want to buy a house."

East's eyes widened. "What do you want to buy?"

I looked at my brothers, at the five of them that were my best friends. Between them and our youngest sister Eliza, there were seven of us. All named with an E, and all different in the same way. Somehow all six of us brothers had joined the Air Force and had rarely lived in the same place. It was hard enough to find a position that worked for you in the military for long, let alone finding a place that was near one of your siblings. It just didn't work out that way. I had been on tour at the same time with at least one sibling, but we were never stationed in the same place. They did that on purpose, from back in the days when wars would take out entire squadrons, and therefore an entire set of siblings. But I still felt like it had been years since I'd really gotten to know my brothers. Now we were all in the same place, *retired*.

Evan didn't want to be here, but I knew it wasn't because of family. No, he had his own reasons for not wanting to move back to San Antonio. We had lived here before when we had been kids, the seven of us, and it felt like home when we'd been little. We could have moved out west to where our uncles had lived on the winery, but that hadn't felt right. Now we were here in Texas trying to make our own home.

San Antonio had enough bases, so many military people retired in the area. It was gorgeous, decent weather if you liked the heat, and it was within driving distance of hill country, wine country, desert, city, and even the beach if you wanted to drive around five hours. It was a good area, and I was glad that this was where we were putting down our roots.

Although, Eliza wasn't moving down with us. When the guys and I had all planned where we were going to retire, I had always assumed Eliza would come with us. And then she had lost her husband in an IED explosion, the catalyst for why all of us Wilders had gotten out when we had.

Between Evan's accident, and Eliza's husband's, we hadn't wanted to stay in anymore. I had reached my twenty while the others hadn't, but we were all out. Though Eliza had found love again somehow and was up in Fort Collins with her husband's family. I didn't begrudge her for that, and I knew we would all be visiting our little sister often, but it was still odd that she wasn't going to be with us.

Either way, though, we were here—the Wilder brothers. Evan was growly and not exactly pleasant at the moment. It had nothing to do with his pain, though, and all to do with his past.

Everett liked it here, at least from what I could tell. He was the quietest of us all, and sometimes it was hard for me to figure out exactly what he was thinking at all times.

Elijah was out of his depth and angry but always had a smile on his face. He was also the only one that actually liked wearing a suit, so maybe he would like what I had in store for us. I wasn't sure, though.

East knew what he wanted, though he never told us. He was growly, a little abrasive, but considering what he used to do, it worked for him. But I knew he needed roots, needed to settle with us, and so that's why we were here. To keep him safe. To keep all of us safe. Including Elliot, the youngest of the brothers, though still older than Eliza by a couple of years. He had gone out earlier than all of us for his own reasons. And I knew of all of them. He was going to click with what I had in mind more than the rest. At least, that's what I hoped.

"Seriously? Why are we here?" Evan growled and then let out a sigh.

I figured I might as well tell them what my plans were, even if they felt insane. "I don't plan on living in this house for long. It's a rental, and I do want to buy. Just not a house."

"You said that, but what do you mean?" Everett asked as he leaned forward over our meal.

"I want to buy land."

They blinked up at me, and Evan tilted his head. "You want to be a rancher? Or just buy land with a lot of oaks?"

I snorted, thinking of the land for sale around us. The market was hot and many people moving out here wanted the land for privacy, not necessarily for what it had been used for in the past. "The place I'm looking at has a few oaks, but not a ranch. No, I want to buy land that is far more expensive than what I can afford alone."

They all looked at me then, while Elijah leaned forward. His normal smile tilted down, and he frowned. "You mean the inheritance? From our uncles?"

Our mother's brothers had both passed within the last year, and we were the only family that they had. When they died, their winery had been sold, as required by the will, but the proceeds from it, as well as whatever holdings they had, went to *us*. Meaning we had a decent nest egg on its way, and none of us had been expecting it or planning on it. So I had plans of my own. I just had to hope that they agreed.

"There's a piece of land that I want to buy. And I want to make it a retreat. Or, rather, continue the property as a retreat with our own touches."

"What the hell are you talking about?" Evan snarled.

"Yeah, you want to spend money that we don't have yet? I mean, I know it was out of the blue, but what the fuck?" East put in.

I held up my hand. "We all need something to do. Right now, we're working in dead-end jobs to give us an income and to pay our bills, but none of us were expecting to get out when we did." I looked at all of them, and they swallowed hard, nodding.

"It's hard to find a new career when you thought you already had one," Elijah whispered. Elijah had been a meteorologist for the Air Force, but the degree he had finally been able to get wasn't in meteorology. It was hard to find a job in the field that he was trained in when he didn't have the right degree for a civilian. But he was brilliant in more than that, and I hoped he realized that.

"Just let me finish," I began. "I want to open up a retreat. A Wilder Retreat. And the land that I'm looking at, the land I've already spoken to the owners about, is a place where we can make it an inn. Host weddings, and there's even a winery attached. The owners are fine with wanting to change the name of the company, too. I wouldn't have done it if they'd had a strong connection to it. We can make Wilder fucking Wines." They all looked at me like I was insane, and maybe I was. But I had plans. "Before you think I've lost my mind, I've been talking to Roy."

"Roy, wait, didn't he open up a place like it outside of Austin?" Everett asked, frowning.

"He did. That's where I got the idea. We all need something to do, and we've all been living on our own and away from each other for long enough that it feels like we're not even the same brothers anymore." They were all silent so I kept going. "I want us to work together. I want us to start a business."

"The Wilder Retreat," Evan growled. "What's our tagline? Let loose and get wild?"

I ran my hand through my hair, knowing our dinner was getting cold, but I had started about this the wrong way. "Fuck I don't know. But we plan things. We can do this."

Everett moved forward. "We're military. We trained in explosives and planes. We don't do wineries or fucking weddings or winery tours."

They were all saying things I had gone over in my head countless times, but the thing was, we were more than our past, and I had to hope to hell we figured that out. "I know that. But we can learn. The place that I'm looking at, the owner is an older man who wants to sell, and there's already staff in place that know what they're doing. We can fit in, find our way. We are more than just the jobs that we were given and trained for all our lives. We can do this. And we need a normal."

"And this would be a normal?" Elliot asked, but I saw the interest in his eyes.

"What do you want us to do for the rest of our lives? Work a desk job? Work for someone else? We've been working for someone else our entire lives. Let's work for ourselves. Let's make it our business."

"What would we do?" Evan asked, his voice low.

"We'll split the business. Each of us would have our own concept of what we're doing. We've all been in charge of organizing and setting up plans and strategizing. Our jobs as teens were like this, even if it's been a few years for some of us. Now, instead of the way that we operated in the military, we'll put it to use for running an inn and a winery."

"I like the taste of wine. I don't actually know how to make wine," Evan whispered.

I shook my head. "Of all of us, you know the most about wine. You worked with the uncles over our summers as a teen and even again every time you visited on whatever vacations you could take over the years."

Evan scowled. "Yeah, so I know a little bit, but I don't know enough to begin a new wine. I only know about the grapes from their place, not these."

"We are near Fredericksburg. They make great wines," Everett said, his eyes narrowing. Everett was brilliant. If he hadn't gone into the service, I knew he would have been an accountant or his own CEO or CFO. I knew he'd be the one to make sure that we didn't go bankrupt. He just didn't know it.

"Evan, they have a vintner, a winemaker. But they need someone to help as the Director. What

Uncle Leo used to do and what you trained for before you joined up." Evan scowled at me, but it didn't look as menacing at least.

"So, what, we each get our own position and we figure out how to work together?" East asked, growling. "I'm good with my hands. I can build things. I don't want to work in hospitality or with fucking grapes."

I nodded tightly. "I know that East. So that could be your job. Things break down, and we need to build things. I have all this written out, and I was going to talk it over with you. But first, I want to make sure that's something that's feasible. On top of that, Roy invited us to a wedding."

"We're not fucking wedding planners," Evan growled.

I held up my hand. "That's why we would hire a wedding planner for that part. As for an event planner? I think we all know who among us could be that person. We could be the people that show off our area. To plan tours for the winery, or even downtown San Antonio, or anything for when somebody wants to relax. We have spent our whole lives working for the government, risking our lives. Now, let's enjoy it. Enjoy a home that we can build. And help others relax, too. I know it's insane. But I didn't want us to work together in a bar or build a company from the ground up. This place is already settled, and it has potential. We can hire someone for the wedding part, someone good. But we can do the rest."

"And Roy wants you to visit him then?" Elijah asked, speaking of my friend who had gotten out a couple of years before me, and had sparked this idea.

"He has a very similar concept a couple of hours from us. I want to see how it works, and you should come with us."

"So, we're going to crash a wedding?" Everett asked.

"Well, I was thinking you and I could. And at least take some notes. Everyone else has to work, and I figured some of you guys might not be in the mood for a wedding."

Evan grunted, and we all knew who I was talking about at that moment.

"This is insane," Elijah began, but held up his hand when I started to interrupt. "But I could see it. We've all talked about getting out and working together. We just happened to get out far sooner than we planned."

There was silence in that, but we were good about not talking about the whys of it.

"So we're going to start over, work for ourselves,

and we have the money to do this?" Everett asked as he pulled out his phone and started running numbers.

"We do. I hope. I'll send you what I have. The owner doesn't have any kids and wants to sell. He also wants to keep the business that he already has in place operating. He's one of us. Retired Air Force."

That made Evan's lips twitch. "I guess we can listen to him then."

I knew that would get Evan. We were a brotherhood, even those not by blood. I didn't know if this was going to work or if it was just a lark.

I wanted us to be together. I wanted us to work towards a common purpose. And if that meant going out on a limb and trying something completely crazy and something that could risk everything, then I would do it. We had risked our lives for longer than I cared to admit. Why not risk something else to find a home?

In order to be settled.

Everett and I could see Roy and realize that this wasn't what we wanted, and we'd find something else. This had shown up out of the blue, and it just spoke to me.

I was probably losing my goddam mind, but I didn't have anything else.

I wanted my brothers settled, and I was the eldest. I needed to make sure that they were safe and had a future. None of us were married, other than Eliza. None of us had a family. We had spent so long protecting others. Now it was time to think for ourselves.

So we would. And I would make sure that they had a path—that they had a future.

First, however, it was time to go to a wedding.

Chapter Two

Alexis

My job was to plan. And yet, I didn't think I could prepare for this.

"I just really wanted the sun to shine from the goddess on my wedding. And yet it feels as if she's crying." The bride paced in front of me, her hair in hot rollers, her eyes puffy from sobbing. I risked a look behind her at the bright sun and the single white puffy cloud in the sky. The cloud that was apparently sending this woman over the edge.

"It will be okay. The weather is still on our side."

I knocked on wood as I said it, knowing that's what she wanted me to do. And frankly, I would have done it anyway.

"Do you see that cloud? That cloud is mocking me on this day. It is mocking everything that I have stood for. Now how will I know if my love is true, knowing this cloud exists? I was supposed to be wed. To blend my soul with that of my mate and to know that our forever was only a beginning. And yet, it is over. Everything is over." She flung herself on the chaise lounge while her mother glared at me before patting her daughter's arm.

"We'll find a way to make this work. I know it's going to be hard, but don't you worry. We will find a way."

The bride began to sob in earnest. "Today was supposed to be about love and prosperity. I saw it happen."

I nodded even though she couldn't see me and knelt by her, putting on my best wedding planner tone. "Of course, it's about love and prosperity. You are going to marry the love of your life this afternoon."

"Will I? Or will that cloud ruin my destiny? For I was told that today was the day that we were supposed to be married. I saw it in the cards, as did my psychic. Don't you see? She told me today was the day."

I sat back on my heels and nodded sagely at her words, trying not to roll my eyes. I was of the mind that people were allowed to believe in whatever they wanted to, that there was more than one possibility for the world we were in.

And yet, right then, it was all a little too much for me. Mostly because everything had been planned by me, and therefore the psychic. The psychic had chosen this day for the wedding, so I had agreed to it. The psychic had read what color the wedding needed to be in tea leaves, so I had gone with it. My job was to make sure the bride was happy, and the groom as well, but mostly the bride in this case.

The groom just seemed happy that his bride had said yes after years of trying to get her to commit, and therefore I was here. To work on the Baylor Ranch and Brewery and to plan this wedding.

I truly loved this venue. Roy Baylor, the owner and operator of the retreat and venue was a wonderful man, a little strict, but knew what he wanted. And that meant making sure that the bride was happy.

Even if a single cloud in the sky was about to ruin her day, apparently.

"Okay now, let's think about what this cloud can signify," I began as my assistant walked in, her eyes wide at the scene in front of her. I waved her off, and Emily slowly backed out of the room, trying not to make a noise so she wouldn't get caught.

At least she was allowed to leave. Maybe she would be able to work with the caterer, the venue, and to ensure everything else was on track for the wedding that was supposed to begin in forty-five minutes.

I smiled softly and did what I did best: made the bride happy. "That single cloud can be evidence of the path you were once on. The path of you as a woman. But it is showing you that you are ready for the next phase. To the blue skies that will be your marriage." Emily gave me a thumbs-up as she walked out, and I did think that I had done pretty well just then in terms of making crap up.

"Do you think? Do you think that Reggie will be okay with this? That he won't leave me because of this cloud and what it can signify?"

I leaned down in front of Phoenix and held her hand. "You are a beautiful bride. Exquisite. You are marrying the love of your life. I cannot wait to see you in that dress and to watch the reaction of the love of your life as he sees you for the first time today."

She patted her lip, her pout slowly decreasing. "It is a beautiful dress."

"And you are the beautiful woman in that dress. He is going to marry you, not because of the signs, but because he loves you. And that cloud is not the shadow upon your day. It is just a mere moment in time, signifying it is the next phase of your life. It is time for you to marry your Reggie. For Reggie and Phoenix to have a wedding on the books like no other."

I wasn't lying then. This would be a wedding like no other.

"Do you think?" she asked as her mother continued to wipe tears from her face.

"I do. Now let's get you finished with your hair and makeup. And then in that dress. Reggie's waiting. Much like that cloud was waiting for you to see it so it could depart, and you can know that your day is in perfect harmony."

One of the bridesmaids rolled her eyes, and I gently narrowed mine, warning her not to say anything. She grinned wide, and I ignored her and went to help the bride finish getting ready. Knowing she was in good hands with the rest of the wedding party, I went to my other duties, focusing on the caterer and whatever else came up.

The best man walked past, his face a little too bright, and I leaned forward and handed him a mint and a bottle of water from the side table. "Eat this and drink this. No more pregaming before the wedding."

He smiled at me, a little sloppily. "Yeah, I know. I'm just trying to walk it off."

That was good to hear, at least. "No worries, we will make sure that this wedding is amazing. Just stay a little more hydrated."

"You've got it, boss. Thanks, Ms. Alexis."

I waved him off. "It's what I'm here for."

The venue had its own florist and caterer, so I didn't have to use my contacts, which was nice. Not all venues had that, nor did they have their own planning stations. I liked working with places like that felt as if they were resorts. Those didn't tend to have an on-hand wedding planner, but an event planner where I could step in and do my part of the job. Sometimes it got a little hard to mix the two, but Jeff and I worked well together. Right now, he was working on another event for the company while I was working on this wedding. Some guests at the resort weren't part of the wedding itself, and so it was Jeff's job to make sure that they had something to do that would not interfere with the wedding. Now mine was all about the ceremony and following reception. I checked over the cake one more time and made sure everybody was in their place.

"Blue alert, blue alert," Emily said into my headset, and I held back a sigh.

"Blue?" I asked as I made my way to her.

"It's not quite urgent, but it does have to do with the color of the bridesmaids' dresses," Emily whispered fiercely as I came to her side.

"What is it?" I asked, and then I didn't need her to explain.

One of the bridesmaids, Jasmine, if I remembered correctly, was not wearing the correct dress. Oh, it was the right color, but it used to have far more fabric than it currently did.

"Crap on a cracker," I mumbled.

Emily blinked. "Is that the saying?"

"It is now. Okay, let me handle this." I rolled my shoulders back and smiled as Emily went to deal with another part of our checklist. I looked at Jasmine as the other woman just narrowed her gaze, put her hand on her hip, and showed off a generous amount of leg.

"You can't tell me what to do," Jasmine snapped, and from there, I knew that the other woman had planned this on purpose because she wanted to be the showcase of the day.

Well, screw that. This was what I was good at and what I was going to fix.

"You look wonderful, Jasmine. Though the dress is a little bit different than what we had planned on, correct?"

"Oh, I had always planned on this. Phoenix has always been a little too much. You know? This will put her down a peg."

I smiled through my teeth, even as my eyes went cold. Jasmine must have seen the look because her hand fell, and she raised her chin defiantly. "Today is about Phoenix. And Reggie. And their love for one another. While you do look amazing, this is not the dress you agreed on."

"There's no way you can add more to it. I've already had it altered."

I nodded tightly. "Oh, I know. However, when there's a will, there's a way."

I looked to the side as Emily came running

forward, our seamstress right beside her. "Now come on, I know exactly what you need to do."

"There's not enough time," Jasmine snapped.

"Arabella is brilliant at what she does. We'll make the time."

Arabella's eyebrows winged to the top of her forehead as she took in the gown. "It's a good thing I've brought extra fabric. You never know when you're going to need to add an entire skirt."

The defiance on Jasmine's gaze didn't alter. "You will not be touching me or my dress."

I raised a brow. "And if you continue to think that way, you will not be in the wedding."

"This is not your day. You don't get to tell me what to do." Her lower lip wobbled and while I wondered what might have happened between the two women in the past to lead them here, my job was to ensure the bride was happy without hurting anyone in the process. Finding that balance was a tap dance.

Thankfully I'd taken lessons.

"No, this is Phoenix's day. And actually, I do get to tell you what to do. This is not the same dress that the others had decided on, therefore, you will have to wear something appropriate for Phoenix. I'm not going to tell you what's appropriate in general or in life, just what the bride wants. And today is about what the bride wants."

"She's just going to get divorced in a minute anyway. She and Reggie aren't even good for each other. He liked me first."

This wasn't something I was going to get into. I didn't have it in me. Nor did I care. I turned toward the seamstress and gave her a genuine smile. "Thank you, Arabella."

Arabella grinned. "Don't you worry. I'll get it taken care of."

"You're not listening to me," Jasmine snapped, and I tilted my head and smiled at her, knowing it didn't quite reach my eyes.

"Today is not about you. Or me. This is about the bride and the groom. This is their moment. You don't get to ruin it. Even if you might feel differently. When it is over, you can have a lovely talk with Phoenix, and I will understand. But for now, you will fix your dress, you will walk down the aisle and smile, and you will be the beautiful woman that I know you are, inside and out." That was stretching it a bit, but with the way that Jasmine's eyes warmed slightly, I had to hope that that was the right trick. "You can do this, Jasmine. You can show the world that you can handle anything."

"He was mine," Jasmine murmured.

My heart hurt for her, even though I was slightly cold inside when it came to love these days. Not that I was going to mention that. "But he's hers now. And you said yes to the wedding. Be a good friend. Show that you love them both."

"Fine," Jasmine snapped and turned to follow Arabella.

"That was one disaster levied," Emily whispered just by my side, and I nodded tightly.

"We'll keep an eye on her."

"I'll do that since you have the other thousand things to do."

I shook my head. "We'll do it together. We have twenty minutes until go time. Time to go through our checklist one more time."

We nodded at each other then went to work, fixing the maid of honor's shoe and then the flower crown for the flower girl. The ring bearer currently had his finger halfway up his nose, so I helped wash his hands and anchored him to one of the groomsmen who could handle the kid. I walked from pew to pew, ensuring that each flower arrangement was where it needed to be, and as the minister nodded at me, a gentle smile on his face, I knew we were almost there.

So close.

Roy stopped me on my way to the bride and grinned. "Good job, Alexis."

I smiled at the older man and shook my head. "Not yet. Almost there, though."

"Of course, can't put the cart before the horse and all that."

"You sound more and more Texan every day." I winked.

He let out a rough chuckle. "I try. Now, I'll see you after the wedding. Save me a dance."

I rolled my eyes, knowing Roy was happily married but was doing his best to try to get me out on the dance floor because apparently I needed to have a life. I had a life, thank you very much. It just didn't have anything to do with weddings. Other than the fact that my entire life was weddings. Just not my own.

Once the wedding began, I had my eyes on every person that I could at the same time, narrowing them at Jasmine as she walked in her now full gown, Arabella's magic to die for. Jasmine looked like a princess herself, a little manic, but didn't ruin the wedding. And when Phoenix walked down the aisle underneath the blue skies—without a single cloud—I smiled and let out a relieved breath.

The first part was now over, now for the actual reception where things were just getting started.

My photographer was set up for photos, and I let Emily handle half of them when I ensured that the rest of the wedding guests were doing their thing in the reception. They were going for a buffet, so people could mingle and party about, and the dance floor would be rocking soon. First, though, we had a few other things to handle, and I was exhausted. I should probably sleep a little bit more before big weddings, but I had too much on my plate.

When the bride and the groom made their entrance, I smiled, and Emily wiped away a tear.

"They're just so beautiful."

"They are," I agreed. I also didn't think they would last long, but maybe they would surprise me. I liked when they surprised me. I wanted love to last, even though sometimes it didn't, and it broke you.

Emily nudged me, and I looked over at her, shaking my head. "What? Is something wrong?"

"Look over at *them*. All tall, dark, and handsome. And growly. I want to take a bite of that. Who are they?"

I laughed. I couldn't help it. One of the guests gave me a look and smiled, and I held back a wince.

My job was to blend into the scenes, not to make noise and laugh. I had to be better than that.

I stared over at the two men with dark hair and blue eyes and frowned. I didn't recognize them, and I had to wonder what side of the wedding they were from. I frowned, going through my mental list, but figured they had to be someone on the groom's side since I didn't know everybody by their face. However, they seemed to be brothers and were attractive, though I didn't swoon like Emily seemed to be doing. Barely.

"Seriously though, who are they? And are they single?"

"You can find out after the wedding. We do not mix pleasure with business. You know that."

Emily put her hand over her heart and mimicked it beating while she fluttered her eyelashes at me. "Don't you wish we did, though?" she purred, and I shook my head before I met the gaze of the slightly older man. His blue eyes intensified and narrowed on mine before a shiver went down my spine. I swallowed hard, and broke the connection, and looked down at Emily.

"Not for us. You know that."

"Spoilsport. But I suppose we have to get back to work."

I swallowed hard and then looked back to where the man had been standing, only to find the space empty, and sighed. "Time to work. It's what we're good at."

And I pushed the thoughts of the man with the blue eyes from my mind, knowing I had far more important things to worry about tonight.

Chapter Three

Eli

"Why did I say I'd wear a tie?" Everett asked as he worked his collar.

I snorted and looked over at my younger brother. "Because it's a wedding and its formal, and we were told by Roy we *had* to wear a tie. It's not my fault you borrowed Elijah's rather than buying one for yourself."

Everett sighed, worked his collar again. "I know I'm going to need to buy an actual suit that fits if we do this. It's also not my fault that I looked damn fine in my dress blues, but my shoulders outgrew my old suit. Hell, I'm going to be the CFO, damn it, I should look the part."

I held back a grin, knowing that Everett might be growling slightly at the plan, but I knew he was in. Of all of my brothers, he was the most into it. That was Everett. Quiet sometimes, but determined.

"You're in then? CFO and everything? You've got the background and the degree for it."

Everett gave me a look, a single brow raised. "Of course, I'm in. I was in when you first mentioned it, even though it sounds insane."

I held back a laugh since I didn't want to draw too much attention to us. "I guess that would make me CEO. Though I don't want to think about being your boss."

Everett shook his head. "You've always been our boss. You're the big brother. The only one you couldn't order around is Eliza, but then again, none of us can order around our little sister."

That made my lips twitch, and I took a sip of the champagne the waiter had brought about. I wasn't a huge champagne fan, but it tasted good, and I felt like I needed the liquid courage to be here. It was odd to be somewhat crashing a wedding, though Roy said we could come as observers. We weren't going to eat or draw attention to ourselves, but it was good to watch what Roy and his team were doing. I knew there was a wedding planner around somewhere, one that Roy hired on since he didn't have one on staff. However, Roy was thinking about hiring someone permanently.

If the Wilders did go along with this insane plan, we'd be following Roy's footsteps to the letter.

"I don't know how to take that. Am I bossy?"

Everett grinned. "Yes. You're colossally bossy. It's what you do. Then again, you were the only officer among us."

I shrugged. "I got lucky with a scholarship and placement right out of high school, and things worked out for me. I was also in longer than any of you."

"And now we're all out, a bunch of NCOs without jobs."

"Local accounting jobs at the warehouses not doing it for you?" I teased.

"I hope that this works out because I'd rather you be my boss than anyone else. Yeah, you get annoying sometimes, but you're my brother. I wiped your brow after you threw up after too many drinks. I feel like that connects us."

I snorted. I couldn't help it. "You did that for

East. He's your twin. Not for me. I'm a little too old for that."

There was a seven-year age gap between the twins and me, even more so between Elliott and me and Eliza. There were seven of us, and honestly, not too many years between us. I didn't know how my parents had done it, and never got a chance to ask before they died.

"Think we can do this?" I asked after a moment, looking at the party in front of us.

"Plan a wedding? No. Do everything else? Yes, I think we can."

I looked at him then, my eyes wide. "Just like that."

"Not just like that. You had notebooks and files on what it takes. And we're going to that workshop about inns and owning your own business."

"One where Roy promises it's not a timeshare scam." We both laughed at that before I continued. "We'll learn, and we've got the money to do it. I mean, I guess we could use the money for other things, but this is for our future, not just for a new car or new house."

Everett's lips twitch. "Considering most of us will end up living on the property if things work out well, it *is* a new house. And we've got decent cars.

And there'll be enough after we buy the place to hopefully to get a new truck or two since we'll need it. For hauling."

"And because we live in Texas and need to fit in," I said with a laugh.

"And you know that Evan is going to thrive on the winery side."

I swallowed hard at Everett's words. "He will. If he lets himself."

"That's a big if. But, hell, he's the one who worked with the uncles for the longest. He's the main reason that we even had this opportunity. Not that we can let him know that."

I smiled despite myself. "You're right. We could figure things out but he's the glue. We each have a job. Each have a purpose. We work together. We wouldn't split up, take too much time away from each other like we've been doing for twenty years. Hell, I left the house to go pursue my own future when you guys were babies."

"I wasn't a baby. Sure, Eliza was, but I wasn't."

My lips twitched. "Close enough since you were like in puberty."

Everett sighed, looked over his shoulder. "Please, say that loudly for the people on the other side of the ball ballroom."

I looked around the vast room with the elevated ceilings and twinkling lights. "Our ballroom won't look like this."

"True, but ours would be in a renovated European-style farmhouse. The place is in good shape. It's like a fucking villa."

I snorted at the look of one of the guests at our cursing. "That was the goal for the original builders. They wanted to bring a little bit of Europe here with the architecture. So it is a villa of sorts in the middle of south Texas."

"Well, this is a little more upper-class farm."

I nodded. "We won't be competing for each other, even though we're a couple of hours away."

"Which is a good thing because we like Roy and need his help. We don't want to piss him off."

"Why don't you want to piss me off?" Roy asked as he walked over to us. Roy was a big man, mostly still muscle after all these years as a civilian, and he took care of himself. His hair was graying at the temples, and his full beard was white and gray now. He looked good, and he had been my friend for years. We had fought together, had been neighbors and even roommates for a bit in our early years. He was a couple of years older than me, so he got out before I did, but we had stayed in touch and, hopefully, he'd be able to help me figure out exactly what the hell I was going to do with the rest of my life.

"We were just thinking about taking your business," Everett said with a grin, and Roy just threw his head back and laughed, that big deep laugh that made everyone around us smile. Nobody glared at him. He was just the good guy who people got along with wherever he went.

Maybe that's why he was so good at this. I wasn't that guy. Whatever it was. Everett was. As was Elijah. And Elliot. East, Evan, and I were a little more on the asshole side of the family. But half of us being assholes, the other half being decent guys wasn't a bad mark.

"You're welcome to try, though. I think with the winery on your side and the brewery on mine, it's a good fit. We'll be able to send whoever can't fit into ours to each other. Working like a partnership, rather than adversaries."

The way that Roy said it, it seemed like a decree, and frankly, I agreed. "Sounds good to me. And honestly, it'll be nice having footsteps to follow in, even if we're trying to be our own bosses."

"I had footsteps too. The guy who owned this before I was a retired general."

"No shit?" I asked.

"Two star. Wanted something with his life a little bit different, and this was in the family. He sold it to me, and now you're buying from a former military man as well. It's all in the family, even though our family's a bit convoluted."

"Don't even begin on the whole convoluted family thing," Everett added with a grin.

Roy let out a big belly laugh that drew a few gazes our way. "There are seven of you, all starting with the same letter. What the hell was your mother thinking?"

I just smiled, used to the refrain. It had been worse when we'd all been active duty and went by Wilder. "We answered to numbers mostly. I was one."

"I don't remember my number. I think mom forgot it too." Everett said with a grin.

Roy leaned forward, laughing. "Well, you're a twin. I'm sure you and East switched off often just to annoy your parents."

"I can neither confirm nor deny."

Roy just grinned. "Well, you've had a look around. You saw the books and figured out what we do. What is it that you want?"

Everett looked to me, and I swallowed hard, rolling my shoulders back. "We want something that we can work together in. The place that we're looking at we would rename to Wilder Resorts. It has a good flow. It just needs some updating, but we can do that. Especially within the budget. We're already in talks, and they're not talking with anybody else right now for selling, so that's a good thing."

"Time is still on your side," Roy added.

"For sure. There are twenty cabins outside of the main building. The main building is a villa, with its own atrium and dining room and breakfast room and all that. The innkeeper can live there. And then within the cabins, we can designate some of those for the family like they did, so we can live on the property and not have to pay rent or mortgages on other places."

"That makes sense. We live in a house on the property. If you live in those cabins, are you going to cut into your bottom line?"

I shook my head. "No, this is what the other owners did before us with their teams. It makes sense. And while we all did training for other things when we were active duty, all of our degrees went towards what we thought we'd do as civilians versus what we did in the service. Oh, and we can take the cabins that need the most work for ourselves and work on them on our own."

Everett snorted. "Thanks for giving us the heaps to live in."

I raised a brow. "You've seen our land. There's nothing heap about it."

"That is true," Everett whispered.

"There's a pool, a sunning area with a shit-ton of tile that's perfect for photos according to the owner's daughter. And then, on the other side of the acreage, there's a winery with forested trails. There's a tasting room, barrel rooms, a large building for all the equipment. It's like its own business on the property."

Roy nodded along as we went over everything again. "And it's a lot of acres, more than I have. But then again, you need more land for the vines. Not that it's a huge heap of vines, but a respectable amount for good wines in moderation."

"It's a shit ton, but pricing right now is good, and I think we can make it work."

"I'm here if you need me, but it's a good opportunity. Yeah, it's different than what any of you guys did in the military, but hell, most of us were just handed an instruction packet once we joined, after we took a test to see what we were most suited for. Not that we knew what we were suited for, and then we went into that field. You can do that here."

I nodded. "We can. And hell, this might be nice. Something completely different."

"You're jumping into hospitality, think you can do it?"

I sighed, looked at my brother. "I think I want to."

"I don't think, I know." Everett grinned and then reached out and squeezed my other shoulder.

"Now to convince the others." That made me wince but Everett looked unfazed.

"They're not going to need convincing," Everett said with a tight nod. "They're already excited. Or at least as excited as they can be with their scowls."

"I sure do love your family," Roy said with a laugh. "And look, the garter toss is about to begin, go boys, go see if you're the next to get wed."

I blinked, looked at Roy. "I thought you said we needed to be casual observers."

"True, but there aren't as many single men here as there are single women, so go stand over there and fill the place so that way it's not three guys vying for a garter."

"Isn't that kind of archaic?" Everett asked, and I snorted.

"What he said. I'm not going to go catch a fucking garter."

"Go. Stand there. Don't hold out your hands. Just stand there and look forward. Fill up the space."

"I don't understand you," I grumbled.

"You don't have to. You just have to do what I say."

"He did outrank you," Everett said with a grin, and I flipped my brother off before I lowered my head at Roy's glare, and walked over to where the dozen or so men were standing, hands in pockets, looking for all the world they would rather be anywhere else.

"They needed men for this, my ass," I grumbled, and Everett snorted.

"Hey, look on the bright side, the odds work in our favor now that we won't catch it, which is good. We have enough on our plate without getting married."

"My mom forced me over here, so I'm going to hide behind you," a man in his early twenties said as he smiled over at us. "If that's okay."

"Fuck no, you're not hiding behind me. I don't want the damn thing," I growled.

Everett just grinned, the asshole. "Nobody does, but here we are, at a place where love and happy ever after is the only thing that matters."

I shook my head and stood there, hands in

pockets as the bride sat down on a chair, and every-body started to cheer. Music began, and the groom went down on his knees, slid his hands up the bride's dress, and slowly, very slowly took her garter down.

"Well then, I feel like we're part of a peep show," Everett mumbled out of the side of his mouth, and I elbowed him to keep him quiet. He let out an oof, and when the groom stood up, swung the garter over his head, I held back a sigh. Apparently, we would have to get used to this, because a big part of the income were events and weddings on the property. I was going to have to start enjoying shit like this if this is what I wanted to do with the rest of my life.

Everybody started shouting, laughing, and I looked up as the garter was flung from the groom's hand and slapped me directly in the chest. On instinct, I reached out and gripped it and blinked.

"Fuck," Everett said with a laugh as everybody cheered.

"Better you than me," the younger man said before he rushed off to where his mom stood. The kid's mom glared at me, and I looked down at the frilly white thing and just shook my head.

"Well, shit," I grumbled.

"Oh, look at you, you're the next to be wed. I'm

so proud," Everett teased as he wiped away a fake tear.

Everybody started congratulating me, and there were a few curious looks, probably wondering where the hell I had come from. I was supposed to be lowkey for this wedding, and here I was catching the fucking garter.

We moved out of the way as the bride came back, tossing bouquet in hand. "Okay single ladies, let's see who's going to get a ring on it!"

I held back a groan at the cheesy joke and watched as a few dozen women all lined up, jokingly ready to fight for the bouquet.

My gaze caught the eyes of one woman as she stood off to the side, earbud in her ear as she looked around at the others. This had to be the wedding planner, the woman that I had seen before and nearly swallowed my tongue over.

"You're drooling," Everett whispered.

"She's hot. Can't help it."

"And she's not for you. Remember? We said no dating."

"When did we say that?" I asked as I shook my head.

"You're gone, just like that, one look, and you're gone."

I didn't answer. Instead, I watched as the bride tossed the bouquet, but she sort of twisted her body as she did so, laughing and probably a little bit drunk. The bouquet flew over the heads of the rest of the party and slammed into the wedding planner's face. She caught the bouquet, her eyes wide, and looked beyond mortified.

"Oh my God, I love it!" the bride screamed. "I knew the tea leaves said this. I knew it! Now, where's our garter man. We have to see the dance!"

I met the gaze of the wedding planner, and then I looked down at my garter and then back up again.

"Well shit."

Chapter Four

Eli

I SHOULDN'T HAVE BEEN SURPRISED WHEN ROY'S hand pressed on my shoulder and practically pushed me towards the woman holding the bouquet.

"Dance! Dance! Dance!"

The crowd cheered, egging us on, and I found myself standing in front of the wedding planner, her soft blue suit nearly gray, and noticed that it was also a dress of some sort. She looked regal and yet like she wanted to blend with the background—something I should have been doing as well.

"This is not happening," she mumbled under her breath, and my eyes widened.

"Nice." I hadn't meant to say that aloud, but damn, I was the only one who was supposed to not want to be there. Not her.

She blushed and looked up at me. "Sorry."

The bride moved forward, her eyes bright and a bit manic. "Dance! Come on, Alexis. It's my wedding. And I want you to dance, darling."

The wedding planner leaned forward, and I tried not to inhale her rich scent. "Phoenix, I need to help with the next part of the setup."

"You can do that after you dance." The bride put her smile towards me, all teeth and manic eyes. "And, hello stranger. I don't know who you are, so you're probably with my lovely groom. However, you are about to dance with one of my bestest friends. This is my wedding planner. Wedding planner, this is the stranger."

"Eli. My name is Eli."

The bride gave me another shark-tooth smile. "Good. Eli, darling. Now, dance. Dance for me, my pretties!" she said with a clap of her hands as her groom came forward, rolled his eyes, and pulled her back.

The groom grinned. "Just do what she says, and

it'll all be over quick." He winked as he said it, then kissed his bride's neck, and she let out a little giggle. The two seemed in love, and like they were perfect for one another, even if the bride seemed a little high-strung. However, it was her wedding, so for all I knew, this was just an abnormality.

"Come on, let's just get this over with," the wedding planner mumbled under her breath as she slid her hand into mine.

"It'll be over before you know it," I replied with a grin as I put my hand on the small of her back. Her eyes widened, and I swallowed hard at the feel of her against me. She was all soft and curved, and it was hard for me to focus. Fuck, it was just hard for me in general. She was beautiful. Gorgeous, and she smelled like sin. Or maybe that was just floral perfume. I didn't know, but she was gorgeous. How was I supposed to focus when she was pressed up against me?

"Hopefully, the song will be over soon. I'm sorry. I don't mean to be a jerk, but I do have things to do for the wedding, and I'm not supposed to actually be around and in the spotlight like this."

I swallowed hard as the music turned into something softer, and we danced carefully.

"I should probably tell you then I shouldn't be in the spotlight either."

Her eyes narrowed even as her lips twitched. "Tell me I'm not dancing with a wedding crasher."

"Technically, I was invited. Just not by the wedding party."

She looked up at me, blinked. "You are with Roy then."

I frowned. "I don't know if *with Roy* is the right statement."

She laughed and it lit up her whole damn face. What the hell was with this connection? "You're here to watch Roy and to see what he does because you're thinking about buying something similar. To join the innkeepers and wedding venue circuit."

I couldn't stop staring at her mouth, so it took me a minute to catch up with her words. "I didn't realize he told you all that."

"Of course, Roy told me. We're about to have strangers at the wedding. I should have put it together beforehand, but I've been a little side-tracked. Busy day."

"It sure looks like it. The wedding looks fantastic, though."

"I hope so." She looked around, smiling softly.

"We worked hard on it. And the bride and groom are beautiful together."

I looked over at them as they swayed from side to side, not dancing, just the two of them holding one another off the dance floor. It was just the two of us on the dance floor. Alone. With all eyes on us.

I held back a frown at the thought, even with the warmth of the woman in my arms. "I don't know if I like being the center of attention. I won't be once we run the place."

She smiled softly at me, her eyes filled with understanding. "No, you won't be. And neither one of us should be here in the limelight now."

I grinned. "I won't tell if you won't."

"I think the cat's out of the bag on that one," she whispered, her eyes dancing with laughter. She smelled so good and felt fucking amazing against me. I wanted her. Just like that, I wanted her.

There was a connection there, I could feel it, and from the way that she swayed into me, even though I knew she didn't want to because she was working, I felt like maybe she felt it too. Or maybe that's just what I wanted. What I was dreaming about and imagining.

"You're a wedding planner then. But you don't work for Roy full-time."

"He told you that?"

"Seems like Roy likes talking about everyone in his circles to each other," I said with a laugh.

"Seems like. And I own my own business. It would be nice just to work for Roy, but Roy wasn't sure if he wanted a full-time wedding planner since he has an event planner on hand."

I nodded softly. "We're thinking along the lines of having both. Because my brother Elliot would be great at all the other planning that comes to the resort, and any minute details that would come about. However, wedding planning isn't something we've ever done before."

"And running an entire inn and business like this is?"

"You got me there, but I don't know if Elliot really wants to do that."

"So would you hire on a wedding planner ad hoc, or would you have one on full-time?"

"That's the discussion right now, and we're leaning towards full-time."

She grinned, and I couldn't help in joining her. "Sounds like you guys are planning well."

"If this weekend goes well, we sign on the dotted line on Monday."

Her eyes widened, even as my heart raced. I

didn't know if it was the thought that we'd be spending a shit-ton of money on Monday or that smile on her face.

Damn it, I didn't have time for this or complications, and yet I wanted her.

There was something seriously fucking wrong with me.

"Well, I think Roy said this would be a couple of hours away, so not exactly in my jurisdiction as it were, but I know some people. I'll make sure you get my card afterward."

"I see, you just want to give me your number?" I asked, teasing. I surprised myself by even saying it since that wasn't normally like me, but she just smiled at me and shook her head.

"For work, buddy. I *am* working."

The song began to shift to something else as people came out onto the dance floor, joining us, and I almost hated the interruption. But the connection didn't snap. It didn't go away. It was still there.

"That's our cue. It was lovely meeting you, Eli. And I will get you my card." She paused. "For work."

"Whatever you say. The wedding is gorgeous."

"Thank you, and I hope you sign on that dotted line on Monday. I don't know. I just have a good feeling."

So did I, but I didn't say it. At least not then.

I followed her off the dance floor, ready to see if she wanted a drink, even if she was working. I couldn't help it. Everett gave me a weird look, but I turned and kept my attention on the woman I couldn't keep my mind off.

That was when I noticed the man in the slick gray suit, fancy haircut, and wide smile on his face come up to her.

She stiffened for just a moment.

"Clint," she whispered as she pushed her honey-brown hair back from her face. Some of it had fallen from her bun and made her look far more disheveled than she was.

Clint. Well then. Either this guy was an ex, someone she didn't want to meet, or someone that was going to ruin any plans that I had.

"Baby. I talked it over with the bride, and well, you are amazing. I love you." He went down to one knee, and the bride started to squeal, clapped her hands as everybody started to murmur in hushed tones, either cheering or with wide eyes.

I looked at the man on one knee in front of the woman I swore I'd had a connection with, at her wide eyes, and held back a sigh.

Fuck.

I turned to see Everett there, his own eyes wide. "You know what, let's do this. Wilder Resorts. We can do this. The six of us. We'll figure it out."

My brother cleared his throat. "I know we will. And what about the girl?"

I held back a snort as we made our way through the crowd, people cheering around us. "Clearly not for me. I don't need a woman. We all know what happens when we let our guard down.

"Yeah. We do."

And with that, I left the wedding alongside my brother. The two of us ready to meet with the other four and plan the rest of our lives. We had shit to do. Things that were all Wilder and just for us.

And I pushed all thoughts of a wedding planner, a bright smile, and a connection that clearly hadn't been real out of my mind.

Chapter Five

Alexis

I STOOD TRANSFIXED AS MY BOYFRIEND OF TWO years knelt in front of me in his Armani suit, and I just blinked. Mortification slid over me, embarrassment slamming into it.

"Clint," I whispered fiercely, wondering what the hell he could have been thinking. *This was someone else's wedding.*

Not only were public proposals tacky, but they were also the worst things in the history of all wedding planning. *You never proposed in public.* What if the person wanted to say no? What if things got weird? Because they were already really fucking weird.

I loved Clint. I truly did. I knew we were going to get married.

But how could he not know me well enough to understand that a public proposal at a wedding I was working at would not be a good idea? Why did he think that that would be a good idea?

"Baby. I love you. You plan all the weddings. You put everyone else's needs and happy ever afters in front of your own. Now, baby, it's time to plan your own happy ever after. To plan ours."

I just blinked at him, my mouth going dry. "Clint."

"I know you're looking at me like I've lost my damn mind. Maybe I have. But I love you. I've already talked to the bride and groom. You know I work with him."

"Oh. Right."

Why couldn't I say anything longer than a word or two? Why couldn't I focus or breathe? Why couldn't I do anything other than want to run away but unable to do so?

"I love you, Alexis. I want to spend the rest of my life with you. Here on the happiest days of two of my friends, they gave me permission to ask you to make me the happiest man on this earth." I looked over his shoulder sharply at the bride and groom as they held each other, tears flowing down the bride's cheeks. She gave me a thumbs-up and mimicked drinking tea, and I wanted to pass out. Over and away.

She had seen this in her tea leaves. Of course she had.

I looked to the right to see Emily rushing towards me, her mouth gaping open, her eyes wide.

I saw the look of *what the fuck* on her face, and it mirrored my own.

However, if I walked away, if I broke down and broke Clint's heart right here, I would be the bitch of all bitches. I would ruin this wedding and put a pall over everything. Nobody would ever want to hire me again. I would lose my job. Lose my sanity. I would lose everything.

This man, the love of my life, had proposed to me in the worst way possible for a wedding planner, but he seems so earnest about it.

I couldn't ruin this day for anyone.

I wanted this, I reminded myself. I wanted happiness.

Clint was mine. He was my forever.

We might as well start now and not ruin everything that I had worked towards along the way.

I lean down, and whispered, "Yes."

He beamed as he went to his feet and cheered, "She said yes!"

"Champagne for everybody!" The bride shouted out, and the room cheered, clapping each other on the back and laughing and taking photos. Clint cupped my face and kissed me softly.

"I knew you would love this. I knew this was perfect."

I looked at the man that I loved, at my fiancé, as he slid the ring onto my finger, a ring I didn't even notice because I couldn't breathe, and had to wonder if I had just made the biggest mistake of my life.

Want to see exactly how Eli and Alexis make it back to each other?

Read their romance in ONE WAY BACK TO ME!

A Note from Carrie Ann Ryan

Thank you so much for reading **A NIGHT FOR US!**

Alexis and Eli's romance is only beginning. Want to know what happens next? Start the Wilder Brothers with: One Way Back to Me!!

If you want to make sure you know what's coming next from me, you can sign up for my newsletter at www.CarrieAnnRyan.com; follow me on twitter at @CarrieAnnRyan, or like my Facebook page. I also have a Facebook Fan Club where we have trivia, chats, and other goodies. You guys are the reason I get to do what I do and I thank you.

Make sure you're signed up for my MAILING LIST so you can know when the next releases are available as well as find giveaways and FREE READS.

Happy Reading!

The Wilder Brothers Series:
Book 1: One Way Back to Me
Book 2: Always the One for Me
Book 3: The Path to You

More to come!

Want to see exactly how Eli and Alexis make it back to each other?
Read their romance in ONE WAY BACK TO ME!

Inked Kingdom

I fell for Sarina the moment I saw her.

When the Kingdom tore her for me, I promised revenge.

My claim was forfeit the moment she ran, but now I will follow.

I will find her.

I will earn her.

And I will burn the world if they dare touch her.

Again.

Chapter Six

Stone

The fist slammed into my jaw, the crunch of flesh to bone echoing in my head. I stumbled back and tried to fight, but the person holding me back tightened their grip, my arms pinned behind me.

"Fucking take it, Stone," the man in front of me grumbled as he hooked his fist out again, this time connecting with my ribs.

I let out a shocked gasp, annoyed with myself for doing it. Eddie's eyes narrowed into slits, the glee in them familiar. Eddie loved doling out pain and seeing others fall.

The fucking bastard. The fact I'd broken just the bit that I had would egg him on, and I had been doing so well not saying a damn word. As long as I didn't make a sound, Eddie would get tired and stop.

Now he wasn't going to stop anytime soon.

Fuck.

"The King already told you what you could fucking do with your retirement, Stone. You think you're too good for us? The King *made* you. He took you from nothing. Kept a roof over your head when your own father didn't even want you. When your dear old mother left you to rot in the alley with your brother. The King kept you alive when that rat bastard of a brother finally kicked the bucket as he should have long before. Who the fuck do you think you are?"

Rage ravaged my body, threatening to overpower me and make me lose control. If I lost control, I'd die. I wouldn't be able to face Eddie and keep up with the man behind me long enough to draw in my next breath.

"I'm not a pretty boy like you, it seems," I finally answered, with a smirk of my own, and the man holding me kneed me behind my legs. I let out a curse, and Eddie grinned.

"That's a pretty boy. Look at you, pretending

you're some tough shit when all you're going to do is go cry to your mother." Eddie grinned again. "Oh, you can't do that because your mom is dead. I guess that's what happens when you go against the King. You know she screamed when she died. Bent to save you, and yet it's not going to be enough. She's dead. Now you're going to join her soon. I can't wait to tell the King to send you to meet your mom. She was hot, though. Kind of miss the fact that I never got to tap that."

Fury boiled through me, and I pulled at the other man, at Rook.

His name wasn't Rook. That was his title. Eddie was the Knight. We were part of the Kingdom, its organization outside of Desolation, New York. We ran guns, booze, drugs—anything to make the King richer.

I had been born into the life, I hadn't had a choice.

I might say that I could get out, but there was no leaving it. The only person that had left had been the one person that I'd loved.

Only Sarina was gone. She had been the Princess, daughter of the former Knight, sister of the older Rook, before everything had changed.

Now her family was dead, and Sarina was gone, and I was alone here.

Alone in a city of crime, of terrible choices, no getting out.

Somehow I was going to leave.

I had no other choice. If I wanted to live to see my next birthday, or fuck, see the next sunrise, I needed to leave before the rest of the Kingdom put me in front of the King.

"Fuck you." I growled out the word, knowing I needed to leave. I needed to be who I needed to be and fuck everyone else.

There was no way that I could stay here. No way that I could survive if I stayed with the Kingdom, in New York, or with any attachments to the Ruin.

The Ruin was made up of the major powers of crime and unorder congregated in Desolation, New York. It connected all the bosses, the cartels, the mobs, the games, and the outsiders. Anyone who was anyone in our part of the country was connected to the Ruin.

And I needed to sever that connection if I wanted to survive.

If I wanted to have her.

I had claimed her once, and she had left. Not to

leave me, but to save herself, the one thing I hadn't been able to do on my own.

She ran from me once, from my world, from *our* world, and now I needed to find her. But the first thing I needed to do was get out of their hold.

"You really thought you could do it," Eddie said as he shook his head. He gestured behind me, and I frowned because the man holding me didn't move. No, instead, there was a sound of boots on cement and someone being dragged.

I froze, ice sliding up my veins. I looked at Jeremy.

Jeremy was the single friend I had left in the Ruin. He was a runner like me, but he tended to make poor decisions. Even worse than I did when it came to this life. I didn't do drugs. I didn't beat women. I didn't use anybody other than myself. Jeremy tried his best to emulate that but sometimes made the wrong choices.

Still, Jeremy was my only friend.

Eddie looked at me then and pulled the Glock out of his holster.

"You both thought you could leave?" He shook his head. "Guess you were wrong, weren't you?"

"I swear, I wasn't going to leave. I love the Kingdom. I love the King. I bow before him." Jeremy began to ramble, tears slid from his eyes, and I just blinked, wondering what the fuck Jeremy had done.

Because while I was going to leave, because I had to, Jeremy was supposed to wait. He had wanted to stay. He would never betray me or his King. What the fuck had he done to warrant this reaction from the Knight?

"The King sends his regards, Jeremy. Next time, don't fuck his daughter."

Jeremy let out a scream, and then there was nothing, just the sound of a gunshot echoing between my ears and my stomach falling out.

This couldn't be happening. Jeremy couldn't be dead. The Knight hadn't just killed a man in cold blood in front of me. But of course he had. They'd done it before. And if I wasn't careful, they'd do it again and again until there was no hope.

No salvation.

Jeremy fell, the single perfect precision hit right in the middle of his forehead. Eddie sighed and put the gun back in his holster.

"We're going to have to get the cleaner in here to clean this up," he growled. "Do you want to use ours or someone else's?"

"Call Arlo." Rook chuffed behind me. "That

way, our guy doesn't have to get his hands dirty. Arlo will be good at it."

Ice crawled all over me. Arlo was the cleaner for higher-ups in the Ruin. Nobody knew exactly what he did, but as Arlo worked for the Petrov Bratva. He was a big mean son of a bitch.

Nobody messed with him, and if Arlo was coming here to clean up the mess Jeremy made, he was here to clean me up too.

I swallowed hard, looked at my dead friend, and I wondered how the fuck I got here.

I was such an idiot.

I needed to get out of here. I needed to get out of the life that I had no choice in until now.

I couldn't even feel remorse for the friend that was dead. I didn't have time or the luxury to *feel*. Everything was numb. Hollow. Unending.

Jeremy was dead. And he had cried.

And I was next.

"I think the King wants to do this personally for you, boy," Eddie said as he shook his head. "I'm not going to waste a bullet on you."

Then Eddie moved forward and snapped out his wrist. The taser hit me right in the chest, sending electric shocks down my body. I hadn't even realized that the Rook had let me go, was laughing behind me. I fell to my knees, and then the taser was gone, and they were kicking. Steel-toed boots hitting my side, my ribs. Something cracked and I coughed up blood. And then there was a fist to my temple, and there was nothing.

"Wake up, dumb ass. Open those eyes."

I looked up into the dark eyes of the man above me and figured maybe this was how I was going to die. Maybe the King didn't want anything to do with me after all.

"Come on, before they take you to the hub, the Ruin doesn't need to see your dead body. And neither do I."

"Arlo?" I asked as I coughed.

Arlo looked down at the blood that I had sprayed on his chest and rolled his eyes. "Thanks for that. Come on, let's get you out of here."

"What the fuck?"

"You want out? I got you a car. No questions."

"But how? Why?"

"See, those are questions. And I don't want fucking questions."

"I don't understand."

"You don't need to understand. Just get the fuck out of here, Stone. You want to survive? Leave."

"But what about you?"

"There are different ways to survive, Stone. You know that better than anyone else." He tossed the keys at me, and I caught them with my left hand, my right one still aching from when Eddie had stomped on it.

"What are you going to tell them?"

"Again with the questions. It's like you want to be killed."

He shook his head and walked off without saying another word, as if speaking to me had been too much for him in the first place.

I looked over at the small nondescript sedan in front of me and wondered what the fuck was going on. My head ached, and I had a feeling I might have a concussion, but I ignored it.

I got in the car, started the engine, and wondered if I was trusting the wrong person. After all, I had been trusting the wrong people my entire life. What was one more wrong choice?

I needed to go, needed to find my home. The only home that I could think of was the one who had left me, the one who had needed to run, the one I hadn't gone after.

But there was no time like the present.

My only friend was dead, taken away when I was out cold, and I hadn't even had time to mourn or wonder what I could have done.

My family was long gone, taken from me before I'd had the strength to fight back to try to save them.

All that would be left for me at the Ruin were the death and destruction of whatever the King declared.

So I started the engine and I pulled away, wondering what the fuck Arlo was thinking and how the fuck I was going to repay him.

In the end, it didn't matter because I was looking for her.

For Sarina.

My life was forfeit.

The claim I once had on her long gone.

My past lay in ruins, but she was the one for me.

She would be my salvation.

Or my ending.

Chapter Seven

Sarina

I TOSSED THE RECYCLING IN THE DUMPSTER AND shook my head. Well, standing in an alley surrounded by dumpsters and trash was at least better than my former life. It wasn't glamorous, but it was mine.

My back ached, my feet hurt, but to me, that just meant an excellent job for the day. I still had another shift at the bar later, but for now, being a barista at Café Taboo paid some of my bills.

That's why I worked as a bartender at Ink on

Tap, the gay bar down the street that my best friend owned, in the evenings.

I didn't have a life, but that was fine. Who needed a life when you were working two full-time jobs and sleeping when you could? I didn't need a life outside of that.

At least, that's what I told myself.

After all, I had lived dangerously and a little more high-octane when I had been in high school. I didn't need anything more than this.

I rolled my shoulders and turned towards the other side of the alley to get back into the café and finish my shift. I tripped over a rock, my whole body turning to ice as I looked at the person in front of me.

It was a ghost. It had to be a ghost because he couldn't be there.

After all this time, that couldn't be Stone Anderson standing in front of me. The one person I had left, the one person that had taken everything from me.

Or rather, perhaps I had taken everything from him.

I had given him myself, my innocence, my heart, my future, and he had thrown it away because he chose his family over me.

He had chosen everything over me.

"Stone," I whispered, my voice cracking.

"You remembered me."

I blinked at him, my hands shaking. "What happened to your face?" I asked, wondering why that was the first thing that came out of my mouth. Of course, it couldn't be helped. He looked horrible.

Perhaps beneath the split lip, black eye, and swollen cheekbone, there was still that gorgeous ruggedness that was Stone, but I could barely see it. No, instead, all I could notice were the imperfections, the signs that perhaps he hadn't left the life like he had promised me he would.

He had stayed behind when I left, and whatever had wrapped its hands around his neck had taken more from him that I could comprehend.

"Sarina," he whispered, his voice a growl. It did things to me, just like it always had. That was the problem with Stone.

No matter what I did, I couldn't think when he was around. He made me lose all sense, lose all reality.

Because he was supposed to be my everything. My salvation. My one true everything.

And then he had chosen the Kingdom.

Chosen the place that had killed my father. Killed my brother. Killed everything.

Chosen the place that had wanted me. Not for who I was, but what I could do for them.

They had wanted my body, my soul. They had wanted everything other than who I was and what choices I could make.

Stone had chosen them.

How was I supposed to look at the man in front of me and want anything other than to run?

So I did. I left the alley. I turned on my heel, and I ran.

My feet dug into the gravel, and I ignored the blisters on my heels. I ignored Stone's shout.

I ignored him.

I'd have to call Hailey later and let her know why I had left in a hurry, but she would understand. She had to. She and all of her family always understood what was going on. It was as if they had a sixth sense. They would understand why I had to leave. They might not know every detail, they knew enough to understand my running. At least for the day, and if Stone wouldn't walk away, perhaps forever.

I had been hiding in Denver for four years, but maybe this would be my last moment. Maybe I would have to fully leave and never come back. Never return to the place that I had called home for so long.

I ran down the block, and nobody paid me any mind.

They were all focusing on their own lives, their own problems. Nobody cared about the woman in the apron running for her life.

I had left my purse behind, everything. The only thing I had was my phone, and whatever wits I had left.

Because if Stone was here, the Kingdom couldn't be far behind.

And I needed to be safe.

I couldn't be near them.

Because if the Kingdom found me, I would be dead. My life would be forfeit, as would everything else I had ever thought I could possibly have.

Because once the Kingdom had you, there was no leaving. The King had wanted me for his Queen, even at a barely legal age.

He had seen what Stone had, and had wanted me. His own Queen had died only six months prior, and everyone said it had just been an accident. We all knew that was a lie. The old Queen, Gwen, had been the Guinevere to her Arthur and had found her own Lancelot. She had cheated on the King, fallen in love with the wrong man. With the one man, she couldn't have and he hadn't been ruthless enough to save them.

She died at the hands of her own King, of her husband.

And the King wanted me.

And when I said no, he killed my brother, his Rook.

And when my father, his Knight, had fought for me, he killed him too.

Their blood still stained my palms; I could see them in my dreams, hear their screams. In the end, there was nothing I could do.

I had run. I hadn't run far enough, it seemed.

It was never going to be far enough.

Stone had found me. And soon, the new Rook and the new Knight would as well.

Stone was their runner, their tracker.

And the others would follow, and I would die. Because I would die before I fell before the King as a supplicant.

Before I became his bride.

Before I filled his bed.

I would die.

I pounded on the backdoor to Ink on Tap, praying that Rebel could hear me.

"What the fuck, Sarina?" Rebel asked as he

pulled open the door. He was shirtless and in sweats and looked like I had just woken him up. Maybe I had. It was still early enough in the day that he was probably sleeping upstairs in the apartment that he owned rather than working on opening up the bar. Of course, nobody would be here other than him for the next hour or so, but it didn't matter. I needed to find a place to be safe. I needed to be safe.

"Can I come in?" I asked, my whole body shaking.

Rebel gave one look at me, tugged me in by my apron, and slammed the door behind me, locking it. "What's wrong? Are they after you?"

Rebel had left the Kingdom long before I had. He had dropped out of high school and ran before they could destroy his soul and his heart. That was over fifteen years ago, and now he owned Ink on Tap, the prominent gay bar for the area, the one that was inclusive, a safe house, and a safe place.

It was my salvation, the one place I could be myself.

The one place Rebel could be his self.

And I was going to have to leave it.

"Stone's here," I blurted.

Rebel cursed under his breath. "Is he alone? How did he find you?"

"I think he's always known where I was. Of course, he would."

"Fuck. Okay, we can get you some new identification, get you out of here."

"I left my purse and everything behind. I'm such an idiot. All I have is my phone."

"Okay, we'll get you out of here. I know somebody up in Wyoming. They can keep you safe."

"Really? Is that going to be the best I can do? Running for the rest of my life?"

"I don't know what else we're supposed to do, babe. I'll go with you. So you're not alone."

"You can't give up everything."

"I would. You know I would. My family's long dead and the King won't even remember who I am. After all, he didn't know me as Rebel."

I nodded and sighed. "Okay. I guess I'll leave? I don't know. I don't know what I'm supposed to do."

Rebel opened his mouth to speak and then frowned, pulling out his phone. "Well. It seems that Stone found you. Fuck. Okay, we'll get you out another way. Unless they have us surrounded." He let out a breath. "It's been so long since I've done this. I'm rusty."

Stone's voice came through the doorbell camera alert. "Sarina? I'm alone. I left. I promise you. I left."

Rebel and I both froze, my palms damp, bile filling my throat. "Did he say he *left*?"

"That's what he says. Fuck, it looks like somebody did a number on him." Rebel met my gaze. "Sarina, babe. Stone would never have hurt you. You know that. He might have stayed to protect his brother, but he always promised that he would never hurt you."

"Why are you throwing that back in my face?" I asked, my laugh hollow. "He did hurt me. Just not in the way that he might think."

"Of course he did. He's a man. He's a dumbass. He stayed in the Kingdom to protect his brother, but he's out there, looking pretty hurt, and I don't know, something doesn't feel right about this."

Tension slid up my shoulders again. "What do you mean?"

"There's nobody on my surveillance, Sarina." He showed me his phone, at the eight cameras and their feeds. "Not a single thing. And none of my contacts have warned me that any of the Kingdom's coming here. I'll reach out if you want to see what's going on with Stone, but this doesn't feel like a setup."

"Isn't that going to be the last thing that anybody says before they find out it was a setup?"

"Maybe. But come on, let's go see what Stone

wants. I'll protect you."

"I'm not going to have you hurt because of me."

"It would never be because of you. You know that."

"Rebel, we left."

"And maybe Stone did too."

I swallowed hard and rolled my shoulders back. "Fine, he's never going to go away. It always seems like he can find me. I'll see what he wants, tell him to go, but you stay safe. I don't want him to see you."

"Sarina."

"What? Let me protect you for once. Maybe it's my turn. I shouldn't have come here. I put you right in the thick of things all over again."

"I'm here to protect you. Remember that."

"No, we protect each other." I kissed him hard on the mouth, and he rolled his eyes before he followed me towards the backdoor.

"Stay out of sight."

"Fine, but let me put on shoes. I'm not going to fight off a team while I'm barefoot and shirtless."

"If anyone could do it, it would be you," I teased, trying to lighten the tension.

"Sarina," Stone said again, through the doorbell camera. Rebel had the camera set up to hear what Stone was saying outside, and that was the only reason I felt somewhat like I could have control here. It took me forever to find my control, my own life.

I opened the door partway, the glass partitioning it off. It was bulletproof glass, and there was no way Stone could make it through. At least, that's what I told myself.

"Sarina. You ran."

"Of course I ran. What are you doing here, Stone? I'm not going back."

"I'm not going back either. I'm free." He shrugged, then winced, pressing his hand to his side.

"Stone." I reached up, almost getting to the door to help him, then realized what I was doing.

He wasn't going to get me this way. Nobody was going to make me feel like an idiot. "I'm fine. Just need to heal. It was a goodbye present from Eddie and the others on my way out."

"You're gone then. You just left."

"There was no just about it, but I'm out. I'm not going back." He let out a shaky breath. "I should've left long ago. I was a fucking idiot. But I needed to stay for Phoenix."

"I'm sorry about your brother." I swallowed hard. "I heard about what happened."

"Sorry about a lot of things."

Phoenix had been Stone's older brother and had

died in a shootout with a rival gang. I didn't know the details, only that Phoenix was dead, and the sole reason that Stone had stayed was gone. And yet, Stone hadn't come. I had waited foolishly, as if expecting him to show up and for us to pretend that nothing had changed between us and that he had finally had a reason to stay.

In the two years since Phoenix's death Stone hadn't contacted me, hadn't shown, and that had been the final nail in the coffin of whatever dreams I had once had.

I left the Kingdom because there was only death of my soul and my body back for me with the King. I had left, with a promise from Stone that he would come for me.

And then a single note saying he couldn't because Phoenix needed him had shattered every-thing. Had torn away the fragile bonds of whatever promises we had made to one another.

With the death of Phoenix shocking around our underworld, I had thought maybe I had a chance. Maybe he would come back.

He hadn't. Stone hadn't come.

And so, these past two years, I had found a way to be myself, the person that I was.

Stone hadn't come for me. I had come for myself.

"I came for you; you don't have to do anything. I'm going to stay for a while. Figure out who I need to be. But Sarina? I'm back. I'm here."

I looked at him then, looked at the man I had once loved, and I could see the parts that I had loved before, the parts that I had been connected to, but he wasn't him. I loved Stone Anderson. I had given everything to him, and he had stayed to protect his family, and while I understood that, I needed to defend myself. For once, I needed to do something for myself.

"I'm glad that you're out. But I'm not the same person. I'm not the girl that needed your help to get away from the King. I'm not the girl who watched her father and her brother die. You're free, but I've been free longer. Be safe, Stone. But I'm not yours anymore. And maybe I never was." I raised my chin, then closed the door in his face, locked it, and ignored Rebel's look. Instead, I fell to my knees, my hands ice against the cold metal steel of the door, and let the tears fall.

I had loved Stone before.

And perhaps part of me always would.

He was my past, not my present.

And if I wanted to survive, I couldn't let him be my future.

Chapter Eight

Stone

Thanks to Arlo's intervention, I had been in Colorado and away from the Ruin and the Kingdom for four weeks now. Four weeks of me trying to figure out what the fuck I was going to do.

Sarina hadn't wanted anything to do with me, and frankly, I didn't blame her. I had shown up out of the blue, not knowing what the hell I wanted, and she hadn't wanted me. Had practically shoved me out of the way. And I get it. She walked away, and I probably would've done the same in her case.

I missed her, damn it. Of course, I had missed

her when she left before, when she had gotten out and taken the step before I had. She was far stronger than I was, far stronger than I would ever be.

Not that she would let me tell her that. No, she wanted nothing to do with me, and while I was a bastard, an asshole, I wasn't about to force her into spending time with me. So that meant I had to stay away. At least until I found some form of steadiness.

I didn't go into Taboo or Ink on Tap. Those were the two places that I knew for sure that she worked.

In the past four years, she seemed to have found her place, a set of friends, maybe even a family here.

And I wasn't part of that.

Maybe I didn't need to be part of that. Hell, I wanted to be part of that. She was my goddamn forever, and I just wished somehow she would let that happen. She would fall for me again and not want to let go.

Only, if I pushed, if I crowded in, she'd hate me more than she already did. And considering I knew she despised seeing me, that was saying something.

"You ready to go, Stone?" I shook myself out of my funk and looked up at Luc, my boss.

I had been out of a job, in need of funds, and a new way to start my life.

In a past life, I had once considered becoming an

electrician. I was good at it and can usually rig up anything around me that was needed.

That was what the King had used me for when I wasn't a runner.

So I used the skills I had honed in the business to find a job here.

Now I worked at Montgomery Inc. and was working my ass off.

When I wasn't helping Luc with setting up the electric, I was lifting and hammering and sawing, doing whatever else I needed to do for the company.

An entire family owned and operated this place. It was nice seeing how one member of the family was the architect, the other the lead contractor, and one even a plumber. Luc was the electrician. He had married into the family; his wife Meghan was the lead landscape architect. They built homes and some commercial buildings, but whatever contract they got, they seemed to put their all in, always to code and worked with high-end materials.

They were the real deal, completely the opposite of what I used to do.

I felt like maybe I could find a home here, not that I thought I'd ever actually be able to stay. No, eventually, I'd have to go. Because I knew the King wouldn't let me stay for long. Maybe it was a good thing that Sarina was gone then. That she wanted nothing to do with me, because when the King found me, when he sent his men after the runner they had lost, if he even cared that much, they would find her too, and I would never let anything happen to her.

I was down on the ground, my hands covered in dirt as I lifted a box for Luc, when I heard a familiar voice. A voice that broke me.

I stiffened, even as Luc grinned widely on the other side of me.

"Hey man, we're going to take a break."

I cleared my throat and looked up at the dark-skinned man. "Excuse me?"

"My wife's here."

"Oh."

I stood up next to Luc and wiped my hands on my jeans. "I've met Meghan."

"Yeah, she's pretty great, isn't she?"

Only it wasn't Meghan I was looking at. Yes, Meghan, with her dark hair and bright blue eyes was gorgeous, but she only had eyes for Luc, just like I only had eyes for the girl next to her.

Sarina stood there, her hair piled on the top of her head, her hazel eyes wide as she looked at me.

Whatever color had been in her face from her

laughter earlier was gone. Instead, it leeched from her skin as she stared at me as if she had seen a ghost.

Maybe she had.

I wasn't supposed to be here. I had done my best to stay away. Why the hell was she here?

Luc cleared his throat and looked at me. "I know you're running. We all do. I guess you know Sarina?"

"From a lifetime ago."

When we had been young, foolish, and thought we could take on the world. But in the end, we hadn't been able to do anything. We hadn't been able to save ourselves.

"You know, I almost made a mistake before by leaving and not fighting. You might be trying to figure out who you are, but if you think she's worth it, apologize. Make sure she knows she's the center of your universe. And don't fuck it up."

I looked up at the other man and frowned. "You can tell all that from a look?"

"You can tell a lot of things when you've been there before."

Luc shrugged, set down his equipment, then walked over to his wife. "Hey there, baby."

"Hey there, baby, right back."

They kissed each other like they weren't on their worksite, as if they hadn't been married for years.

"What'd you bring me?"

"Hailey was busy today, a conference downtown had heard about Taboo, and now she's stressed out. She sent Sarina here with our lunches, and I said I would help."

"It's nice to meet you, Sarina," Luc said as he held up his hand. Sarina smiled, but it didn't reach her eyes. After all, she was looking at me, then she shook her head, smiled for real, and took Luc's hand.

"It's nice to meet you. Hailey always talks so well about the family. I'm glad I could finally come out here."

"I'm glad you could too." Luc swung his arm around Meghan's shoulders. "Are you going to join us for lunch?"

"Oh, I should go back. Hailey needs me."

"Okay then, just let me know what you need. I'm going to go take my wife to neck around the side."

"Luc!" Meghan laughed, but she didn't counter that. Instead, she followed him, leaving Sarina and me alone.

"You're here," she whispered.

"Yeah. I've been working here for a bit." I cleared my throat. "I didn't know you'd be here. I know you said you wanted space, and I figured I'd do the one thing I should've done a long time ago and fucking listen to you."

She shook her head and looked down at the baskets around her. "I just brought lunch for the crew. Hailey does that every once in a while. Her bakery is right next to Montgomery Ink. The two families own the business, and they're all close."

"That's cool. Luc was telling me a little bit about it."

"So, you're an electrician now?" she asked as she stared at me.

"I always have been. I didn't do it for the right things."

"No, I guess you didn't."

I shuddered, pushing away thoughts of what I'd been forced to do in the past, because I wasn't that person anymore, at least, that's what I told myself.

"Anyway, I'll leave you be. If that's what you want."

"I don't know what I want, Stone. How are you here?"

"I don't know. I didn't expect you."

"Well, to say that I didn't expect you would be an understatement."

"I'm sorry. For taking up your space. For being here. But I missed you, Sarina."

"It's been years, Stone. I already told you we're not the same people."

"You're right. We aren't. I'd still like to get to know you."

"Really?" she asked, and I could tell she didn't believe me.

"I do. I want to get to know you. I'm here for the long haul, Sarina." As long as they didn't find me. But neither one of us needed to say that.

"I left all that behind me. I don't know if I'm ready to see it again."

"I'm not that person. I left. I should've left a long time ago, but I never crossed *that* line. I was never that guy."

We both knew what I was talking about; there was no need to say the words aloud.

"I was so afraid that you'd be pushed into it. I never thought you'd willingly take that step."

"Sarina," I whispered.

"I'm just so afraid. What if you wake up and realize that you miss that life?"

"No," I said vehemently. "I'm not that guy. I left because I needed to, because I wanted to. Because I missed you."

"Don't put that all on me. Don't say that you left only for me."

"I didn't. I left because I wanted to, because I needed my life back. I stayed because of my brother, and that was wrong, but he's gone. They all are. I don't want to be part of that life anymore."

"That life is long behind me, Stone."

"Good. Then let's start over."

I held up my hand. "Hi, I'm Stone."

She looked up at me, then down at my hand, her body shaking slightly as she sucked in a breath.

"Stone," she whispered. Then she let out a breath, met my gaze, and slid her hand into mine. "I'm Sarina."

"Sarina," I whispered, relief hitting me like a two-by-four.

"I'm scared," she said, with a hollow laugh. "What if you leave again? What if I have to leave?"

"I'm not going to let anything happen to you, Sarina."

"We both know you can't promise that."

"I'll try my damned best. But we're going to start over, remember? I'm just Stone. You're just Sarina."

She looked at me then and shook her head. "I don't think there's anything *just* about that. But we can start over. Because walking away from you hurt, it killed me, and I don't think I'm strong enough to do it again." And so we stood there, as others milled about, and I stared at the woman that I loved, the girl that had walked away, and the woman she had become.

I had to hope this wasn't a dream, that this wasn't going to fall around me.

I knew better.

I had always known better.

I just hoped it wasn't too late.

Chapter Nine

Sarina

My feet hurt again, but this time I still had a slight bounce to my step.

I couldn't help it. It had been a week since I had seen Stone at the job site, since I had told myself that I wasn't making a mistake.

And I wasn't making a mistake. Because I had already made one before, by pushing him away. He had been hurting, had been in pain, and I had pushed him away to protect myself.

I shouldn't have done that. Yes, I was scared. Yes,

seeing Stone had brought back memories of pain, agony, and shame.

He had always treated me well. He had always treated me like I was cherished.

He hadn't forced me to stay behind for him. He had watched me go, had stood back to make sure I was safe.

That's what I had to remind myself.

Yes, he had stayed, no, he hadn't come after me until I felt like it was too late, but he hadn't blocked me in.

"You feeling okay?" Rebel asked me from the other side of the bar, and I smiled at him, this time knowing it reached my eyes.

"I am, ready for the night to be over though, no offense."

He just grinned at me. "Oh, no, because your honey bun is coming to stay with you for the evening. I wouldn't want to stay either."

"Rebel," I said as I blushed.

"Honeybun?" Jeremiah, one of my regulars, asked as I handed him his beer.

"It's nothing," I grumbled, glaring at Rebel. "Stop it."

"Stop what?"

Rebel beamed and leaned forward towards Jeremiah. The two had been having a serious flirt for the past couple of months, and I wish they would just ask each other out already. However, fate was a tricky mistress, and they were taking more time.

"Her old boyfriend is back in town."

"Well, if you broke up with him, it must have been for a reason," Jeremiah said. "We don't want you hurt."

My heart swelled, and I could see it did for Rebel too from the look in his eyes. "He didn't hurt me. I had to leave a situation, and he couldn't come with me."

It wasn't exactly true because he *had* hurt me because he stayed away for so long. Only that hurt was also on me.

It wasn't all his fault, nor was it all mine. Sometimes I had to remember that it was the King's fault, the Kingdom, and the Ruin.

Those who had sent us to a life that we couldn't escape. They were who had hurt us both.

I wasn't afraid of Stone. I never had been. I was afraid of what he had represented, what had almost swallowed us both.

That wasn't the case anymore. I wasn't that person anymore. I had to hope that Stone wasn't that person either.

"Anyway, her ex is back in town, and he makes her smile like that, so I'm calling it a good thing."

I blinked and looked over at Rebel. "Really?"

"Of course. I'd say he's your lobster, but we know that lobsters don't mate for life," Rebel joked.

I rolled my eyes. "Please stop telling me random crustacean facts."

"I'd like to know random crustacean facts," Jeremiah said, his gaze only for Rebel. I looked between the two of them and held back a smile. If crustacean facts and trivia were what was going to bring these two together, I wasn't going to stand in their way.

I cleared my throat. "I'm going to go clean up on the other end, and then I'm heading out. Are you two okay?"

"I think we're just fine," Jeremiah answered, and Rebel rolled his eyes.

"You think that line is going to work?"

"I think I have a few more," Jeremiah drawled when I rolled my eyes. I grabbed my bag from underneath the bar, and headed towards the other end.

I'd have to wear my cross-body bag for the rest of the evening, but that was fine. I didn't want to interrupt them again accidentally. Not when things might be working out.

"Hey," Stone whispered from my side, and I let

out a breath, my stomach tightening. I had known he was there, of course. The hairs on the back of my neck had stood on end, and I always knew he was there.

There was something about him. Something that hurt and ached and made me want to give in.

That was Stone. That was always Stone.

"Hi," I said as I looked up at him, at his deep green eyes, the way his dark hair fell over his face.

He needed to shave, and I liked it. That slight stubble that I knew would scrape rough against the inside of my thighs.

I blushed, wondering where the hell that thought had come from, and from the way that Stone's eyes darkened, he must've guessed where my thoughts had gone.

"When are you through tonight?" he asked, his voice a low growl.

"She's done now," Rebel said, not tearing his gaze from Jeremiah's.

I swallowed hard. "Apparently, I'm done now."

"Good, I'll walk you home?"

"Oh. Sure." Disappointment slid through me. In the week since we had reintroduced ourselves to one another, pretending the past hadn't existed even while it wrapped its claws around our throats, we had gone for coffee, for food, but we hadn't kissed. Hadn't done anything.

Had he wanted to start over completely by just being friends? Or was it something more? Was he just taking it slow?

I wasn't sure, but I couldn't read him, and it killed me.

Because I wanted to know, I needed to know.

I was just afraid if I asked, the answer would hurt.

Just like always, everything hurt when it came to Stone and the Kingdom.

"I have my bag, so I'm ready to go."

"Good. Come on, let's take you home."

I walked out from the side of the bar, waved at Rebel and Jeremiah, who weren't even looking at me, and found myself holding Stone's hand. His palms were rough, calloused, as if he worked hard with his hands, and I couldn't help but imagine his hands on me.

Why the hell did I feel so freaking horny? I had had sex before, mostly with myself, but it counted.

Why was it that every time I was around Stone I swooned and couldn't focus? Why was I always wet when he was around?

There was something wrong with me.

"Where are your thoughts going?" he asked as we walked down the street towards the small set of apartments where I lived. It was ridiculously priced in downtown Denver. However, I was subletting from a woman who wasn't charging too much. I wasn't sure why, and I wasn't going to ask questions, but everything was legal according to Rebel, so I would focus on that.

"What?" I asked.

Stone met my gaze, shook his head. "You're in your head, and I don't know why."

"I think you can guess why," I muttered as we walked up the stairs towards my fourth-floor apartment.

"Okay, so you're working two jobs then?" he asked as I let him inside, feeling as if the space was far too small with him around. He was wide, all muscle, and he filled any room he was in. But right then, it felt like it was more as if I couldn't breathe when he was around. Or maybe I could never breathe when he was around.

"Yes, between both jobs, seven days a week and far too many hours, but they're good to me, and I'm saving up."

"This apartment can't be cheap," he said as he looked around the fully furnished sublet apartment.

There were light colors, a modern kitchen, and a small sofa. My bed was in the corner, as it was a studio and not much square footage, but it was enough for me—more than I ever had growing up. Oh, my father had had a decent home before the Kingdom had enveloped us, but then we had moved into the compound, and I had only been given what they allowed me to have, what the King had bestowed upon us.

Because I wouldn't give him what he wanted, it wasn't enough.

"The price isn't that much. It's a sublet. And I think just good luck."

"It's great. I'm renting a hole in the wall in Aurora, and I'm pretty sure that the rats are bigger than I am, but it works."

I frowned. "I'm sorry. Did you sign a lease? We can find you something better."

"It's week-to-week, which is why it's such a shitty place. I was just afraid at first that I'd have to leave quickly, and I didn't want to sign anything. You know?"

"I do, because you're under the radar, just like I am."

"I hate that we are. I hate that he probably knows exactly where I am."

"I know he knows where I am," I said as I shrugged, setting my bag down. "He always knows. We can pretend and change our names, get a fake Social Security card, and go about all the normal ways to hide, but he'd always find us."

"That's why you never changed your name."

"I changed my last name, but there wasn't a point. He always knows where we are because if he can't find us, he has connections with the Ruin, and they can find anybody."

"There's no hiding unless you're dead."

I hadn't meant to say that, and with the storms in Stone's eyes, he didn't like to hear it. "I'm so fucking sorry."

"There's nothing to be sorry about," I said, shaking my head. "You didn't do anything wrong.

"Then why do I feel like I did something wrong?"

"Now that I think about it, you stayed to protect your brother. You survived because that was the situation we were in. I only got out because you found a way for me. And I think I hated myself more than you for you not being able to come with me."

"Sarina," he whispered as he moved forward, his hands cupped my face, and I let out a breath, the warmth of his skin on mine almost too much.

"I hated myself for leaving you behind. For not being strong enough to stay to fight for us. I know you had to stay. I know there wasn't another choice. I think, though, I hated you more than I wanted to when you couldn't come with me later. When your brother was gone, and there was nothing else."

"He chained me in the basement," he muttered, and I froze.

"What?"

He let me go then and began to pace, and I felt the coolness of lack of his touch.

"He chained me in the basement when my brother died. Beat me, did...well, things. I don't want to go into detail because I don't want to think about it. They were training the new Rook, the new Knight, and I was just the runner. They wanted me to kill this kid, this fucking kid, so that I could take over the Rook position, and I wouldn't." Stone met my gaze. "I wouldn't. And when they killed my brother, there was nothing else for me. I tried to leave, and they wouldn't let it happen. I stayed for as long as I was forced to, and then there was nothing else for me."

"Stone," I whispered.

"A friend helped me out, though I don't think he is actually a friend. An ally that I hadn't realized was an ally until it was almost too late to. He got me a car, helped me get out while I was thinking about just taking the bus to get here to you."

"Because you knew where I was," I whispered, my hands shaking.

"Of course I did. I always knew where you were, because I needed to make sure you were safe. That's why I stayed. Well, part of it. Because I needed to make sure you were safe."

Tears slid down my cheeks, and he cursed under his breath. "Stop it. I wasn't blaming you."

"I know. But damn it, Stone, why did we lose so much time?"

"We don't have to lose any more."

And then his mouth was on me, and I was lost. He tasted of coffee and Stone. I moaned into him, craving him. He was the drug, and I was the addict, and it had been too long since my last hit.

An eternity since my last hit.

I slid my hands up his back, digging my nails into his shirt, and he groaned into me, pinning me against the wall. I hadn't even realized that he had backed me up next to the front door until I was there and I groaned, arching against him. My nipples were hard, pressing against his chest, and he smiled against me. "You taste so fucking good.

Like a memory, sin, and a promise all rolled up into one."

"I could say the same of you. I missed this, Stone. I missed you."

"It's only been you," he whispered, and my eyes went wide.

"What?"

"Since you left, it's only been you."

I swallowed hard. "I waited too. I didn't realize I was doing it, but I waited."

He groaned, his thick cock pressed against my belly. "Fuck. I'm not going to last long."

"Then this first time, we don't have to last. I just need you."

"Deal."

And then he was kissing me again, pulling up my shirt. I tugged at him, ripping at the bottom of his shirt until he pulled back, shrugged off his jacket, and remove the shirt over the top of his head. He was all ink and long lines of muscle. My hands ran over the scar on his chest, the other on his hip, another on his bicep, and he cursed under his breath.

"The only scars I have are the ones of my own making. Ignore the rest."

"Only if you ignore them too."

And I tugged off my shirt, leaving me in my bra, and his fingers went to the scar between my breasts.

"I'll kill him for you."

"No. He's nothing right now. Don't let him in here."

The King didn't matter right now. He couldn't. I couldn't let him be part of this.

I may wear the King's scar on my flesh, but I wasn't his Queen. Wasn't his anything.

Stone growled, and then he kissed me again, and I was lost.

I tugged on his pants, and we each toed out of our shoes, stripping each other gently. We were still standing, my back pressed against the cool wall.

"I need to be inside you," he grumbled as I reached between us, gripping his cock. He was wide, long, and I couldn't touch my fingers as I wrapped around him.

"Were you always this big?" I asked, looking down.

He grinned. "It looks like I'm going to have to refresh your memory." And then he reached down, lifting me by my thighs, and speared into me.

I was wet, soaking for him, and he slid right in with ease.

I looked at him, my breath coming in pants as I

looked down between us, at the way that we connected, his cock deep inside my pussy.

"Stone."

"Fuck, I didn't mean to go so fast, but I slid right in."

"Because I'm always wet around you," I said as I clenched my inner walls. His eyes crossed, and he groaned, kissing me again. And then I wrapped my legs around his waist and urged him.

"Please. Fuck me. We'll make love later, but now I just need you to fuck me."

"Deal." Then he moved, sliding deep inside of me. He slammed me into the wall over and over again, and I arched for him, meeting him thrust for thrust. I'd be bruised later, but then again, as my fingers clawed down his back, he'd carry my mark as well.

And that's all I wanted, for him to carry my mark on his flesh, his soul, just like he had branded me long ago.

He flipped his thumb between us, over my clit, and I met his gaze. My mouth parted, and I came. It was a rush, passion and promise and heat all at once as my cunt clamped around his dick, my entire body breaking out into goosebumps as I came, my head thrown back, my body in need.

Stone bit down on my shoulder, grunting as he followed, filling me as if the both of us hadn't been able to hold back. It was hard, rough, and it was perfect.

It was only then that I looked down and realized he hadn't used a condom.

Stone was the only person I had ever had sex with, and if he was telling the truth, and I had to hope he was, I was the only person for him.

"Fuck, I didn't protect you."

"It's okay. I'm on birth control. I'm clean."

Stone let out a shaking breath, his dick still twitching deep inside me. "I'm clean too. But hell. I need to do better about taking care of you."

"It's okay. It's okay."

And then I kissed him, falling in love with him all over again.

The boy that I'd loved, the man that I yearned for, and the promise I knew needed to be kept.

He was Stone, he was mine, and I had to hope that in these moments we had for one another—that this couldn't be the end.

Chapter Ten

Stone

THE SUN WARMED MY FACE AS I LOOKED UP INTO it and let out a deep breath. It had been a long day on-site, and I was exhausted but still revved. I needed to head home, shower, and then I was going to meet with Sarina. Somehow she had taken me back. It wasn't as if we had forgotten what had happened, but maybe we were just figuring out who we could be now.

I liked working for the Montgomerys. They were good people, took care of their crew, and didn't mind that I couldn't tell them everything.

Maybe it was because I figured a few of them had secrets of their own, or had been through shit the same as I had. But they didn't ask questions. Everything was above board and legal, because hiding from the Kingdom didn't happen. I knew they knew where I was, but they hadn't come for me yet. So that was something I would eventually have to deal with.

The Montgomerys didn't mind that I didn't answer their questions. They appreciated the fact that I did good work and was doing my best to learn.

They did care that I didn't have a truck or vehicle, but between walking, and the city's mass transit, I was making do.

I had never not had a bike or a vehicle. I had always had something. It had been a point of pride for me.

I had left my bike back at the Kingdom, and when I had come here, I had sold the car Arlo had given me, not exactly legal since the car hadn't been in his name either, but it had worked.

The place hadn't asked questions, and I hadn't volunteered anything. I'd gotten the money I needed to get my life started, as well as any money I had on hand, and that was it.

That meant I didn't have a vehicle, I had a shitty apartment, but I was saving.

And, if I was honest, I felt like I was also taking advantage of the fact that Sarina let me stay over.

Her sublet was small but fucking nice.

She had made a life for herself, and I was grateful for that.

If anyone had needed a new way to live, a new focus, it was her.

And she was making it happen.

I was so fucking proud of her.

I knew she was working too hard, and while I was too, I didn't want her to have to.

Maybe I could figure out a way to help her. To make it so she didn't have to work as hard. Not that I figured she'd let me help her. She was so goddamn stubborn, but then again, I wasn't that far off.

That's why I hadn't taken the ride offered when Storm and Wes Montgomery, two of the family members that owned the company, had offered to drive me home. They didn't need to see where I lived, even though they had the address. I didn't need to see the pity on their faces. And frankly, I didn't need the charity. I liked them, but I didn't know them. I needed to do this on my own, even if I might be making a mistake. I had made enough mistakes in the past, didn't want to make any new ones.

I turned the corner, my thoughts on what my next step would be when I heard it.

A single booted foot on gravel, one that shouldn't be there. Because nobody had been following me, I had been alone, and yet the hairs on the back of my neck were rising.

I turned and ducked the fist in the nick of time, but missed the man behind me.

"The King sends his regards," a muffled voice whispered into my ear, and then the fight was on.

Someone grabbed me by the back of my neck and pulled me backward. I stumbled a bit, catching my balance, and stuck my elbow out, hitting the other man in the chest. He moved back, and I punched out, slamming my fist into the mouth of the other man.

It was the Rook and the Knight. They had come for me. They wanted me.

Fuck. I'd been too complacent. No, I hadn't been able to hide entirely, as you couldn't hide from the Kingdom, but they'd still found me. I didn't even have a fucking weapon on me because I didn't want to carry.

But I knew they wouldn't care. I only had my small knife, not even a true weapon, and it wasn't going to be enough. And I couldn't reach it with my hands pinned behind my back, eerily reminiscent of the last time this had happened and I had watched Jeremy die.

Rage filled me at the thought of Sarina being in that position this time instead of Jeremy. I would never forgive myself if she got hurt. I couldn't let them find her. I couldn't lead them to her or have them know that I was close to her again.

I tried to get away but froze as the feel of a blade nicked at my neck.

"I wouldn't move, boy. You never know how clumsy I can be."

"Fuck you," I grumbled, knowing if they were going to do it, they'd have already killed me. They were just waiting. For what, I didn't know, but it had to be something. They wanted me, and now they were going to get me.

I just couldn't let them have Sarina.

"You shouldn't have left. The King wants your head, and he gets what he wants."

"I'm not your fucking pawn. I never have been."

"Really? Because you never moved up in the ranks. Never had enough dick to make it happen."

I snorted. "You don't want to hear about my dick, boy."

"That what you're going to go with? Well, too

bad you're going to die out here all alone. Kind of sad, really. Then again, you always were. Couldn't keep your woman, couldn't keep your friends or family. You already have one foot in the grave, Stone. You shouldn't have run out on the King."

"Fuck. You."

I spat out the words, blood seeping from my cut lip, as the Knight hit me again and again, the Rook holding me back.

I couldn't do much, not with a knife at my throat, but I knew they couldn't kill me, not here out in the open.

At least, that's what I'd hoped.

"What the fuck is going on?" a familiar voice called out from a passing truck. The tires squealed as the brakes slammed, and then the Knight cursed under his breath.

"You're lucky this time, boy," he spat, literally spitting in my face.

I growled, and then the Rook let me go, the knife easily tucked away in his pocket.

They ran, Wes and Storm coming at me. "What the fuck? Stone? Dear God. Come on, let's get you to the hospital."

I shook my head, wiped my mouth with the back

of my hand. "I'm fine. They didn't break anything." I winced, rubbed my side.

"At least they didn't rebreak my ribs."

"Jesus Christ, Stone." Storm shook his head. "You need to see someone."

"I can't. You know why."

They might not know the details, but they knew why. I had kept my secrets on purpose. So I wouldn't go anywhere, but I was damn grateful to see Wes and Storm right now.

"Are they going to come after you again?" Wes asked, his hands on his hips as he glared in the distance.

"I don't know. They should give me space, but hell, I just don't know." I let out a breath, defeat lying heavy on my shoulders. "I won't come back to work. I won't put your family in jeopardy."

Storm frowned. "That's not what we said. We're worried about you."

"What about your family?"

"They didn't jump you on-site. They jumped you around the corner because you're walking home alone. We just won't let that happen again."

"What do you mean? You're going to fight back whoever tries to jump me?"

"No, we'll just make sure you're not alone."

"And for how long?"

"Till they give up? We don't know," Storm growled. "It's not like this is something we're used to, Stone."

"I figured that. You guys shouldn't have to deal with me."

"You shouldn't have to deal with this either. It looks like you're trying to start a new life with your girl out here."

"I'm not a good man, you guys." I swallowed a lump in my throat. "I never have been. Maybe I'm just getting what I deserve."

"Well, that's just a crock of shit," Wes added. "You got out. You do good work here. And while I don't want to hurt anyone, I don't want you to get fucking hurt."

"Well, they found me anyway."

"Did you use your real name on your paperwork?"

I nodded. "They'd have found me no matter what. Might as well not get you guys in trouble."

Wes and Storm met gazes and nodded tightly.

"I know someone that can help," Storm added, and my brows raised.

"Excuse me?"

"He's a friend of the family, at the other part of Montgomery Ink."

"What the hell do you mean?"

"Best not to ask questions. We'll see what we can do to make sure that they know you're off-limits."

"What kind of shit do the Montgomerys get into?" I asked, blinking.

"As I said, don't ask questions." Storm shrugged, and I looked between the twins, wondering what the hell I had gotten into and why I felt oddly safe.

"Now get in the fucking truck, and we'll take you home."

"Can you take me to Sarina's instead?" I asked, my voice low.

"Need to check on her?"

"Yeah. And just, well, you know."

"We do," Wes whispered under his breath, and I got in the back of the truck, wondering how the hell I had met these people and how my life had turned into this.

They dropped me off in front of Sarina's building, and I said my thanks, wondering if I would see them again. They said they had people to help? Maybe. Or maybe I had gotten a concussion, and I was dreaming all of this.

Nobody gave me a second look as I walked up

the stairs, and I didn't know what to think about that, but I ignored it. My lip was bloody, I knew I would end up with a black eye, but I didn't look too bad, I figured. I had tried to clean myself up in the truck, but in the end, Sarina would know exactly what had happened.

I should have just gone home. I shouldn't show her this again. What the hell had I been thinking? Maybe I had gotten a concussion.

I turned on my heel to walk out and the door opened and Sarina's voice soothed my soul.

"Stone? What happened?"

I turned, swallowed hard. "I should go home."

"They found you," she whispered, before she tugged on my wrist and pulled me inside. She closed the door behind her, locked the three deadbolts, and put her hands on the door, shaking as she rested her forehead on the metal.

"I shouldn't be here."

"Did they follow you?"

I shook my head, winced. "I don't think so. Wes and Storm scared them off."

Her eyes widened as she looked at me.

"Sarina," I whispered, and swallowed hard.

She moved forward and cupped my cheek, her gaze filling with tears.

"You're hurt. They found you."

"I'm fine. They jumped me, but I'll be more careful next time. Or, I don't know, Sarina. They're always going to be there. There's no hiding."

"I know, I've always been on the lookout, same as Rebel. There's no living your own life if they don't want you to."

She tugged me to the barstool and then pulled out an extensive first aid kit.

"This brings back memories," I said softly.

Her lips quirked into a sad smile. "I know. We've done this before. I did this for my father. My brother. I watched them die, Stone. I watched it all. I don't know if I can do it again."

She reached out, wiped the blood from my lip, and then cursed.

"We can fix it."

"How?"

"I don't know. But I'm not that man anymore. You're not that girl. We'll find a way out. We're already halfway there."

"Halfway there, and yet it seems like we have so much further to go. I can't watch you die, Stone. I can't have our past come back."

I tugged on her arm and pulled her close to me, holding her as tightly as I could without hurting either one of us. "I don't know what I'm going to do, what we can do. I'm never going to let them hurt you."

"What if we don't have a choice, Stone?"

I swallowed hard, but I didn't answer. Because I would die before I let them hurt her, or I would kill anybody who got too close.

What was another mark on my soul, after all?

Chapter Eleven

Sarina

My hands kept shaking as I made coffee. That wasn't the best thing for someone who worked at a café as a barista. But I needed to focus. I needed to work, make money, and maybe find a way for Stone and me to leave again.

It was so odd to think how quickly the two of us had become a pair again. As if no time at all had passed between us, and yet all the time had passed.

I let out a deep breath, opened and closed my hands, and did my best to focus.

Hailey was next door with her husband, delivering drinks to the tattoo artists while I was left operating the espresso maker, working on a latte for an order. The rest of the staff was friendly, welcoming and didn't ask too many prying questions. I had always found that slightly odd since they tended to ask and pry with everyone else. But maybe it was because they knew I couldn't answer. Or at least give the answers that they wanted.

The Kingdom was watching. In the back of my mind, I had always known that. It was why I took the precautions that I could and why I always felt as if I needed to be two steps ahead. The fact that the Rook and the Knight had been here, had come all the way from Desolation, New York, worried me. I didn't know if they had truly gone back. What if they hadn't? What if they were waiting for us to make a mistake again?

I didn't know what I would do if I lost Stone. Or if I lost myself.

I had been honest with Stone before. Falling into a relationship might have been the worst mistake of my life, but walking away from him hurt just as much. Because I loved him. I loved who he was and how he made me feel.

So somehow, not being able to find a future, or at least look into seeing who we could be, pained me.

This wasn't what I had signed up for. This wasn't what I thought I could be, but now here we were, there was no going back. I had taken Stone into my bed and had brought him into my heart long before he had come to Denver to find me.

"Are you okay?" Hailey asked as she moved forward, her hand on my wrist.

I looked up at her and blinked, and gave her a watery smile. "I think I didn't get enough sleep."

She met my gaze, and I wasn't sure she believed me. It was the truth, but not why I felt like this.

"Okay, well, if you need anything, you let me know. I'm here."

I swallowed hard. "Thanks for everything."

"Why does that sound like a goodbye?" Hailey asked, her voice soft.

"It's not."

I swallowed hard. At least, I don't think so.

"Your shift was over twenty minutes ago, Sarina. Why don't you head home? Take the afternoon off from the bar."

I shook my head. "That would be nice, but I don't have the option of doing that."

"No, I don't think you do. You work so hard, Sarina. But I hope you know we think of you like family here. You and Stone."

I frowned. "Really?"

"Of course. Stone works for the other Montgomerys, just like we're family with these Montgomerys. I know this is probably invasive even to mention, but I heard about what happened."

I froze. "What did you hear?"

Hailey winced, and it was such an odd expression on a beautiful face. "I heard that Stone was hurt. That Wes and Storm found him. I'm glad that they found him. And while I don't know all the details, my husband said that things are being taken care of."

I shook my head. "I can't talk about it, Hailey."

"I know. I just want you to know that we love you, and we're here for you. Don't run, okay? We'll help keep you safe."

I met her gaze. "I don't think you know who you'd be fighting to try to keep me safe."

"No, I don't. It's completely out of my wheelhouse. I'm here if you need me. And if you do need to go, know that you can always come back. This will always be your home."

She squeezed my hands and then she walked away. I sighed, knowing I needed to leave. Maybe I needed to leave town. It might be safer for those that I had come to care for. But where would Stone and I go? And would I even go with him?

He had been back for two months, we had been together for only a month of that time, and he had already been hurt.

The Kingdom had already come to Denver after so long of leaving me alone.

Was it because Stone was the last straw? Or had they just been waiting until I had been lulled into complacency?

I wasn't sure, but I needed to make a decision.

I grabbed my bag and walked out of the back alley, heading towards Ink on Tap. My senses were on alert since I was afraid that *he* would find me any moment. The King hadn't wanted me in ages. Maybe this wasn't about me. Maybe it was because Stone had left without permission. Hopefully, the King would forget Stone eventually, and someone else would make a mistake. Or another club or group would anger him, and he'd focus all of his attentions on them. That was what had happened with me, and it had given me over four years of relative peace. I might have been constantly on edge, but that was the path I had been set on from birth. The path I couldn't walk away from.

"Sarina?"

I turned, my hands outstretched, my taser in my right hand, and I looked up at Stone.

He held both hands up and cursed under his breath. "Fuck. Sorry, the bus was late, and I came here to walk you to the bar."

Relief speared through me, and I threw my arms around him, careful not to accidentally tackle him. "You scared the crap out of me."

"I can see that. I'm glad you have your taser."

"Who knows if it'll ever be enough," I whispered, and I kissed him softly.

"I hate that you're so on edge, that you're so afraid."

I shook my head. "You're in the same boat."

"Maybe. You were safe before I came here."

"Was I? Or was I just led to believe that?"

"I don't know, baby. Let's get you to work. Maybe Rebel will hire me too." He winked at me, and I grinned.

"He's always looking for a bouncer. It is a gay bar."

"Hey, I'll have you know I will protect anybody in that bar. As long as you're safe."

"I missed you," I whispered as I leaned into him.

"I missed you, too."

And I knew we both weren't talking about the afternoon and morning that we hadn't seen each other. No, it had been a long four years, four years in which we'd had to stay apart to keep each other safe, and it had taken me a while to realize exactly why.

We turned the corner, and Stone let out a shout. I hit the ground as he pushed me down, covering my body. Gunshots rained above us, and I screamed, trying to cover Stone as well, but there was no use, nowhere to hide.

We were slightly behind a dumpster, but it wasn't enough.

"As I said, the King wants you back. You don't get to decide to leave."

Stone growled, pulled me back from the ground, and I ignored the sting in my palms from where I had hit the gravel and now bled.

"Stay here."

"No," I shouted, my throat tight. I gripped his wrist. "Don't go."

Stay safe.

"They're going to kill you."

"No, they're going to kill you," I spat.

And then we were surrounded. They had guns, knives, and they came at us.

"You really shouldn't have left. And to think, you had had everything. A home, food in your belly, protection. And then you left." The Knight looked over Stone's shoulder. "Left to find her. The little bitch the King doesn't even want anymore."

I should have felt relief at that, but I couldn't, not when this could be the end.

The Knight came forward, glaring at Stone.

"You always were a little bitch, just like her."

I moved without thinking, aware that only the Knight had a gun in his hand. Everyone else seemed to just have knives. Not that there was anything *just* about that.

I moved forward, my taser out, and I got him in the belly. The Knight let out a shocked scream and hit the ground.

Stone cursed under his breath, pulled me back, and kicked the gun underneath the dumpster.

"Run," he yelled at me as the others moved forward, shock in their gazes that I would be the one to do that.

The Rook came at us, knife out, and Stone moved quickly, faster than I had ever seen him move before. He gripped the Rook's wrist, twisted. The other man let out a shout. The knife fell to the ground with a clang, and then Stone punched him hard in the face.

Another man came at us, and I kicked out, using

the training that I had had from self-defense, and kicked the other man in the balls.

I tugged at Stone, knowing we needed to get away, but there were too many of them.

They couldn't get the gun, but they had knives, and I wasn't sure a taser was going to be able to get all of them.

I looked at Stone, so afraid I had made the wrong choice, that he would die and it was going to be my fault.

The Rook came at us again, the Knight still twitching on the ground, and then the most sacred sound in the world came.

Sirens hit my ears, and Stone and I froze, hands up in the air as the police came, then their words shouting at us to freeze, to not move. The alley filled with the authorities, and Stone and I went to our knees, trying to explain what happened.

Considering the way that it looked and the fact that Rebel and Hailey came out, her husband and the other tattoo artists with her to give their explanations as well, I knew that we would be okay.

The King was going to lose some of his inner circle, at least for the moment, but we weren't going to die right then.

Somehow.

I looked at Stone, my eyes wide, and prayed that this could be the end. Or at least an end.

It would be too much trouble. That anyone the King sent from the Ruin towards us would be sent right back, worse off. That Stone was out.

That I was out.

My father had lied. And then he had died. My brother had done much the same.

Stone was here. And he had protected me, and he had let me protect him.

I had to hope that this would be it. That this could be the start of our future.

The sounds of bullets, of shouts, of screams would echo in my mind until the end of my days, but maybe this could be the end. Or an end.

And finally, a beginning.

Chapter Twelve

Stone

I'D GOTTEN MY FIRST TATTOO WHEN I WAS fifteen years old. My father had sat me down, and the Kingdom's artist had branded me. I wore their ink on my flesh and their scars on my memories. But not my soul anymore.

I wasn't that man anymore.

It had been a year since the cops had come. Since everything had changed.

The Kingdom hadn't sent another man. We hadn't even heard from them. The Knight was still in jail, the Rook having gotten out on a technicality, but he hadn't come by either. Last I had heard, the King had sent him off, exiled him for failing to get me. For failing to get Sarina.

In the end, it didn't matter because they wouldn't be coming for us anymore.

I had gotten a few more tattoos since, mostly all of them thanks to the Kingdom itself. You wore your ink on your body to prove who you were to those in charge, and I wasn't with them anymore.

The only tattoo I'd ever gotten for myself was a small S hidden among my sleeve.

An S for Sarina, though some had thought it was for me.

I hadn't begrudged them on that or made them think anything different.

Now this ink was for me.

I let out a deep breath, letting the Montgomery behind me have as much space to work with as possible. We were covering up the brands that were from the Kingdom that had nothing to do with my present or my future.

Doing coverups were a lot more fucking painful than the tattoos to begin with, but I didn't mind. If this were my penance to pay for the mistakes I had made in the past, I would freely pay them.

Sarina sat in the next booth over, a woman with

dark hair with pink streaks bent over and working on her back. Sarina was getting ink for herself, not a coverup, like me. She could focus on her future ink and paths, while I still had a long way to go working my way through my sins.

We were making this work for the two of us. Though I wasn't sure what would happen next, we would find a way to make all of this work. We were already well on our way to doing so.

We weren't the people we had been years ago. And for that, I was grateful.

I had been young, rash, and stupid the first time I had been with Sarina.

Now I was making choices for myself, and we were finding our path together.

She wore my ring on her finger and would soon carry my name as well.

She grinned up at me, and I smiled back, ignoring the pain as Austin went over the mark, again and again, doing his best to cover up the sins of my past.

I had fallen in love with Sarina long before I realized what love was.

She had been my salvation, my path, my future.

And now she was the promise I had never meant to make, the promise I had thought a dream.

The Kingdom was long gone. We were never going back.

In the end, however, she was my empress, my queen, my everything.

And I was one lucky son of a bitch.

****

Want more of Carrie Ann's romances?
Try Inked Persuasion

Also from Carrie Ann Ryan

The Montgomery Ink Legacy Series:

Book 1: Bittersweet Promises

The Wilder Brothers Series:

Book 1: One Way Back to Me

Book 2: Always the One for Me

Book 3: The Path to You

The Aspen Pack Series:

Book 1: Etched in Honor

The Montgomery Ink: Fort Collins Series:

Book 1: Inked Persuasion

Book 2: Inked Obsession

Book 3: Inked Devotion

Book 3.5: Nothing But Ink

Book 4: Inked Craving

Book 5: Inked Temptation

The Montgomery Ink: Boulder Series:

Book 1: Wrapped in Ink

Book 2: Sated in Ink

Book 3: Embraced in Ink

Book 3: Moments in Ink

Book 4: Seduced in Ink

Book 4.5: Captured in Ink

Book 4.7: Inked Fantasy

Book 4.8: A Very Montgomery Christmas

Montgomery Ink: Colorado Springs

Book 1: Fallen Ink

Book 2: Restless Ink

Book 2.5: Ashes to Ink

Book 3: Jagged Ink

Book 3.5: Ink by Numbers

Montgomery Ink Denver:

Book 0.5: Ink Inspired

Book 0.6: Ink Reunited

Book 1: Delicate Ink

Book 1.5: Forever Ink

Book 2: Tempting Boundaries

Book 3: Harder than Words

Book 3.5: Finally Found You

Book 4: Written in Ink

Book 4.5: Hidden Ink

Book 5: Ink Enduring

Book 6: Ink Exposed

Book 6.5: Adoring Ink

Book 6.6: Love, Honor, & Ink

Book 7: Inked Expressions

Book 7.3: Dropout

Book 7.5: Executive Ink

Book 8: Inked Memories

Book 8.5: Inked Nights

Book 8.7: Second Chance Ink

Book 8.5: Montgomery Midnight Kisses

Bonus: Inked Kingdom

The On My Own Series:

Book 0.5: My First Glance

Book 1: My One Night

Book 2: My Rebound

Book 3: My Next Play

Book 4: My Bad Decisions

The Promise Me Series:

Book 1: Forever Only Once

Book 2: From That Moment

Book 3: Far From Destined

Book 4: From Our First

The Less Than Series:

Book 1: Breathless With Her

Book 2: Reckless With You

Book 3: Shameless With Him

The Fractured Connections Series:

Book 1: Breaking Without You

Book 2: Shouldn't Have You

Book 3: Falling With You

Book 4: Taken With You

The Whiskey and Lies Series:

Book 1: Whiskey Secrets

Book 2: Whiskey Reveals

Book 3: Whiskey Undone

The Gallagher Brothers Series:

Book 1: Love Restored

Book 2: Passion Restored
Book 3: Hope Restored

The Ravenwood Coven Series:

Book 1: Dawn Unearthed
Book 2: Dusk Unveiled
Book 3: Evernight Unleashed

The Talon Pack:

Book 1: Tattered Loyalties
Book 2: An Alpha's Choice
Book 3: Mated in Mist
Book 4: Wolf Betrayed
Book 5: Fractured Silence
Book 6: Destiny Disgraced
Book 7: Eternal Mourning
Book 8: Strength Enduring
Book 9: Forever Broken
Book 10: Mated in Darkness
Book 11: Fated in Winter

Redwood Pack Series:

Book 1: An Alpha's Path
Book 2: A Taste for a Mate
Book 3: Trinity Bound

Book 3.5: A Night Away

Book 4: Enforcer's Redemption

Book 4.5: Blurred Expectations

Book 4.7: Forgiveness

Book 5: Shattered Emotions

Book 6: Hidden Destiny

Book 6.5: A Beta's Haven

Book 7: Fighting Fate

Book 7.5: Loving the Omega

Book 7.7: The Hunted Heart

Book 8: Wicked Wolf

The Elements of Five Series:

Book 1: From Breath and Ruin

Book 2: From Flame and Ash

Book 3: From Spirit and Binding

Book 4: From Shadow and Silence

Dante's Circle Series:

Book 1: Dust of My Wings

Book 2: Her Warriors' Three Wishes

Book 3: An Unlucky Moon

Book 3.5: His Choice

Book 4: Tangled Innocence

Book 5: Fierce Enchantment

Book 6: An Immortal's Song

Book 7: Prowled Darkness

Book 8: Dante's Circle Reborn

Holiday, Montana Series:

Book 1: Charmed Spirits

Book 2: Santa's Executive

Book 3: Finding Abigail

Book 4: Her Lucky Love

Book 5: Dreams of Ivory

The Branded Pack Series:
(Written with Alexandra Ivy)

Book 1: Stolen and Forgiven

Book 2: Abandoned and Unseen

Book 3: Buried and Shadowed

About the Author

Carrie Ann Ryan is the New York Times and USA Today bestselling author of contemporary, paranormal, and young adult romance. Her works include the Montgomery Ink, Redwood Pack, Fractured Connections, and Elements of Five series, which have sold over 3.0 million books worldwide. She started writing while in graduate school for her advanced degree in chemistry and hasn't stopped since. Carrie Ann has written over seventy-five novels and novellas with more in the works. When she's not losing herself in her emotional and action-packed worlds, she's reading as much as she can while wrangling her clowder of cats who have more followers than she does.

www.CarrieAnnRyan.com